A REVIVED
MODERN
CLASSIC

THE PRINCESS OF CLEVES

D0778405

MADAME DE LAFAYETTE

THE PRINCESS OF CLEVES

Translated by Nancy Mitford

A NEW DIRECTIONS BOOK

Manufactured in the United States of America

New Directions books are printed on acid-free paper.

First published clothbound in 1951

Library of Congress Cataloging-in-Publication Data
La Fayette, Madame de (Marie-Madeleine Pioche de
 La Vergne), 1634-1693.
 The Princess of Cleves.
 Translation of: La Princesse de Clèves.
 I. Title.
PQ1805.L5A72 1988 843'.4 88-12472
ISBN 0-8112-1070-7 (pbk.)

New Directions Books are published for James Laughlin
by New Directions Publishing Corporation
80 Eighth Avenue, New York 10011

FIFTH PRINTING

CONTENTS

INTRODUCTION

IT is sometimes disillusioning to read the lives and become acquainted with the characters of those whose writings have given us great joy, and never more so than in the case of Madame de Lafayette. The Princesse de Clèves and her friends are one of the most delightful groups of people ever described in fiction—young, gay, spontaneous, good, generous and beautiful. Madame de Lafayette was none of these things. Cynical, snobbish, grasping and ugly, she was, however, very brilliant, and as in France that excuses everything, allowances have been made for her both by her contemporaries and ever since.

Marie Madeleine Pioche de la Vergne was born in Paris in 1634. When she was fourteen her father died and her mother married the Chevalier de Sévigné, uncle of the famous letter writer, the Marquise de Sévigné, and guardian of her children. They lived in an intellectual world on the fringe of Court circles, and as they were neither very rich nor very important and Mademoiselle de la Vergne was not very pretty, they had still not found a husband for her by the time she was twenty-two. In those days women seldom married later than twenty and often as early as twelve, so hope had almost been abandoned, and when the Comte de Lafayette, a boring old country bumpkin, negotiated for her hand they eagerly accepted him. He seems to have

been in love, quite excited to show her his castles and properties and to see her enjoying the charms of country life, so as soon as the wedding was over they drove away to Auvergne, where he lived surrounded by the most beautiful scenery in France.

The beautiful scenery, however, meant nothing to poor Madame de Lafayette, to whom every mile of the jogging journey was merely a mile further away from Paris; his castles, when at last they got to them, were ruinous, old-fashioned, and almost denuded of furniture. However she did not repine. She was probably very thankful to be married and to have escaped the convent; besides it was not long before she began to see a way out of her horribly rural situation.

Meanwhile her only link with the world of Paris was her correspondence with the Abbé Ménage, who is always referred to as an amorous pedant, or flirtatious savant, and who seems to have been half in love, not only with Madame de Lafayette but also with Madame de Sévigné and several other brilliant young ladies of the day. It has been pointed out that, at this time, Mesdames de Lafayette and de Sévigné were quite obscure and it was the Abbé Ménage who was famous (for his Latin and Italian verses), but he was one of those characters who are always regarded as half a joke, and Molière finished off his reputation by portraying him as Vadius in *Les Femmes Savantes*. All the same, Madame de Lafayette would have been lost without him during the early years of her marriage, since he wrote her the gossip of the town and sent her the latest books. Her letters to him have

been published recently. They are uninteresting, heavy in style and often disagreeable, but perhaps the Abbé Ménage was not an inspiring correspondent, and we all know from personal experience how much depends on that.

Madame de Lafayette put up with the dull discomfort of country life and the boredom of her husband's company for several years. At last, having done her duty as a wife by giving birth to two sons and one or two stillborn babies, she managed to persuade M. de Lafayette that her health no less than his advantage made it absolutely necessary for her to go and live in Paris. M. de Lafayette had one interest in life—the administration and enlargement of his estates, and he was always involved in complicated litigation by which he hoped to acquire more and ever more land. Fortunately for her, his wife had powerful friends in Paris and never minded bothering them, and she was able to point out with perfect truth that she would be far more useful to him living in the rue de Vaugirard and pulling strings on his behalf, than she could ever be buried away in the castles of Nades, Lafayette and Espinasse, where she always seemed to feel so ill. At last he agreed. He took her to Paris, settled her into her house, put his lawsuits into her very capable hands and went back to Auvergne. Henceforward they lived on the best of terms, seeing each other every two or three years at most, and M. de Lafayette is hardly heard of again; indeed, until modern research proved to the contrary, it was generally assumed that Madame de Lafayette had been left a widow at quite an early age.

Installed in Paris as a married woman of some wealth and great intelligence, relieved of the incubus of a boring old husband, Madame de Lafayette gradually surrounded herself with a little group of intellectuals, the shining stars of which were Madame de Sévigné and the Duc de la Rochefoucauld. Madame de Sévigné, one of the great charmers of history, was eight years older than Madame de Lafayette and had of course known her from a child, as their families were connected by marriage. She had no illusions about her—"I am loved there as much as one can be loved in that house"—but evidently liked her company; it was to the rue de Vaugirard that she flew to be consoled when her precious daughter married the Comte de Grignan and was taken away to live in far Provence. Madame de Lafayette cordially disliked Madame de Grignan, found the continual recital of all her perfections exceedingly boring, and was very much in favor of them remaining in Provence.

Whether or not the Duc de la Rochefoucauld was Madame de Lafayette's lover has been much disputed. She first made his acquaintance through his mistress, the Marquise de Sablé, and was obliged to give herself a great deal of trouble before he began to go to the rue de Vaugirard. In 1662 Madame de Sablé most conveniently took to religion, threw off the ties of the flesh and made a general confession at the Port Royal. After this the Duke visited Madame de Lafayette every day until his death and, as their mutual friend Bussy-Rabutin so truly remarked, "in such cases there is always love, and even when old age has intervened there is still something left

which, in the eyes of the Church, is as inadmissible as love itself." (M. de la Rochefoucauld at this time was in his fifties, then considered as old age, and was besides blind and gouty.) The Duchesse de la Rochefoucauld could not abide Madame de Lafayette who never set foot in her house, much frequented by Madame de Sévigné and others.

Regular members of Madame de Lafayette's salon included the learned Huet, tutor to the Dauphin, Segrais, the poet, Mignard, the painter, the old Cardinal de Retz, and the Marquis and Marquise de Coulanges.

Madame de Coulanges was famous for her *bons mots* and her confessor used to say, "This lady's sins are a series of epigrams." Her husband wrote delightful songs and they were evidently a very jolly pair, too frivolous, indeed, and too fond of food for Madame de Lafayette, who only put up with them for the sake of Madame de Sévigné.

These people went most days to the rue de Vaugirard; others went when they were invited, which they usually were for some spiteful reason and so that they could be laughed at afterwards. The Duchesse de Brissac, for instance, had the face of an angel, but was a pretentious idiot—she "contemplated the essence of her being and spoke a language of such sophistication that nobody understood what she meant." Madame de Maran was a joke with her short hair. Lovely Madame de Fresnoy, the mistress of Louvois, only pronounced those words that suited the shape of her mouth. The Duchess of Northumberland was asked in order to provide an object lesson

for M. de la Rochefoucauld. In spite of being hideous and badly dressed, in spite of her extraordinary manners lacking in any grace, she was loved with an extremity of passion by the English ambassador, Lord Montague. M. de la Rochefoucauld had of late been looking far too often at beautiful Mademoiselle de Sévigné, aged seventeen—no harm in showing him that youth and physical attractions are not a necessity of love.

The Abbé Ménage was not very much encouraged now that Madame de Lafayette had found more fascinating friends, while the great middle-class writers of the day —Molière, Racine, Boileau, Pascal, etc.—never seem to have been invited to the rue de Vaugirard, though their works were thoroughly read and discussed as soon as they appeared. La Fontaine did go once or twice, but he bored and annoyed Madame de Lafayette with his uncouth manners and had to be got rid of; the fact is that like many intellectuals she was at heart a snob, hankered after high society and longed for a place at Court. In this ambition her friends were no help to her—a hindrance in fact—since both the Duke and the Cardinal were old Frondeurs; M. de Retz was completely in disgrace and M. de la Rochefoucauld, in spite of his great name, literary reputation and the fact that his son, the Prince de Marsillac, was a favorite of the King's, was barely tolerated by Louis XIV. He was shown little or no consideration when he went to Versailles, and was not always even offered a *tabouret* to sit on, though this was his absolute right as a Duke.

women must be smart, beautiful, graceful.

Madame de Lafayette, however, had another card up her sleeve. Her husband's sister, Louise, had for a short time been the mistress of Louis XIII, but had very soon repented and taken the veil at the convent of Chaillot, where the King used to go and have long, sad conversations with her through a grille. She became Mother Superior at Chaillot, remaining on very good terms with the Royal family, and various little Princesses were sent to her to be educated, among others Henrietta of England, daughter of Charles I and first cousin of Louis XIV. Many people, including her mother, Queen Henrietta Maria, thought that this child might well become Queen of France, and Madame de Lafayette, true to the principle of "always be civil to the girls, you never know whom they may marry," took a great deal of trouble with the Princess Henrietta, visited her constantly, relieved the tedium of long conventual days with gossip and flattery, and promised that later on she would write a novel with her as the heroine. The Queen of England herself did not hope more fervently than Madame de Lafayette that her little girl would marry the King of France. Unfortunately, when the time came for marriage, Louis XIV thought the Princess too thin for his taste, and had fallen in love with a bouncing Italian girl, while Mazarin, who really decided everything for him, had determined upon that alliance which eventually gave the Spanish throne to a Prince of France, and not even the prospect of being the King's uncle could shake him in his purpose. So Princess Henrietta found herself married

xv

off, not to her cousin the King, but to her cousin Monsieur, the King's brother.

It is always said that Mazarin had Monsieur educated in such a way that he was bound to become a pederast so that, in the then restless state of French politics, the King should not be burdened with a possible rival so near the throne, and if this is true he succeeded perfectly. Monsieur was a pederast. There was not only no rivalry but a lifelong devotion between him and his brother. His wives, however, did not benefit by the arrangement.

No sooner was Princess Henrietta married to his brother than the King forgot that she was too thin and fell in love with her. A few months of great fun ensued for everybody, the King and Madame leading the Court in every kind of amusement, fantasy and folly, never apart and not attempting to conceal their passion. The Queen retired to her prayers and pregnancies, Monsieur amused himself according to his tastes and neither seems to have minded very much, but after a while the Queen-Mother sent for Louis XIV and told him that he was making a scandal. If he must go on with the affair, she said, with the perfect worldly wisdom which she had learnt from long years of daily contact with Mazarin, he had better seem to be courting somebody in Madame's household, Mademoiselle de la Vallière, for instance, and use her to mask his real activities. Louis XIV, whose chief preoccupations in life were always the dignity of the throne and the good of the state, saw that his mother was right; he pretended to be in love with Louise de la

Vallière, and pretended so well that soon he really was in love and poor Madame's day was over. Nothing now remained to her but to have eight children, of whom only two little girls survived her, and to die in agony and terror, poisoned, as she thought, by the Chevalier de Lorraine, her husband's lover. Louis XIV kept a tender feeling for his sister-in-law, and when he was old she came to life for him again in the person of her granddaughter, the Duchesse de Bourgogne, mother of Louis XV, to whom he always showed a most uncharacteristic indulgence.

Monsieur was the typical pederast of all time, but there was no harm in him and he was quite fond of both his wives. When Madame was poisoned, if poisoned she was (the evidence really points to a burst appendix), Louis XIV made careful enquiries to find out whether his brother was supposed to have been implicated, and when he learnt that nobody in Madame's entourage had even thought of such a thing he was greatly relieved. He knew himself that his brother was incapable of it, but feared it might be said that he had done it.

Princess Henrietta, when she became Madame, the second lady of France, did not forget her old friend of convent days. She was unable to give her an official place in her household, as these were all in the gift of the King, but Madame de Lafayette was continually invited to St. Cloud and the Palais Royal, was Madame's best friend and confidante, and seems to have been on consistently good terms with Monsieur. This, then, was her foothold at Court; she assisted at the manifold intrigues

and dramas which occupied Madame's short life and breathed the Palace atmosphere, which she reproduced so vividly in *La Princesse de Clèves*. She fulfilled her promise of early days by taking notes for a life of Madame, some of which were dictated by the subject herself. She assisted at her death-bed and so was able to give, in her *Histoire d'Henriette d'Angleterre,* a first-hand account of what really happened. This very fascinating little book was published in 1722.

After the death of Madame, Madame de Lafayette's great preoccupation was how best to keep in with the Court. She called on the new Madame, the hideous, clever German woman whose letters are such a joy, and who might have been Queen of England (instead of George I) had she not been brought up a Roman Catholic, but did not make much headway with her— La Palatine hardly counted people as human beings at all unless they were of (legitimate) royal birth. Fate, however, had something even better in store. Mademoiselle de la Vallière had retired, sobbing, to her convent by now and the far more amusing Marquise de Montespan was installed in her place; her sister, the Marquise de Thianges, became Madame de Lafayette's great new friend. The Abbé Testu said of Madame de Montespan and her sisters, "Madame de Montespan talks like a woman who reads, Madame de Thianges like a woman who dreams and Madame de Fontrevault like a woman who talks." Madame de Thianges had intellectual tastes; she loved to go to the rue de Vaugirard and enjoy the

torrents of chat which flowed and sparkled there so brilliantly. She loved these witty friends, she saw how much they longed to be brought to the attention of the Court and most good-naturedly devised a way of doing so. On New Year's Day, 1675, she gave an amusing and original toy, which she had designed herself, to her little nephew, the Duc du Maine.

It was a miniature room, gilded, furnished with a bed and armchairs, and shutting up by means of an iron grille; dotted about the room were wax figures portraying Madame de Lafayette, M. de la Rochefoucauld, the Prince de Marsillac, Madame Scarron, Monseigneur Bossuet and Madame de Thianges herself. This charming object bore a scroll with the words: *Chambre du Sublime.* She presented it to the child in front of his father the King and all the court; for days nobody talked of anything else and the group of the rue de Vaugirard was known henceforward as the *"cabale du sublime."* Nothing could bring M. de la Rochefoucauld back into favor, but Madame de Thianges' little manœuvre worked wonders for Madame de Lafayette. The King probably remembered that she had been a friend of Madame, at whose death-bed they had knelt side by side, and now that she had been brought to his attention again he often invited her to royal entertainments, even on one occasion taking her over Versailles himself to point out the improvements which were always going on there. Seeing at once the way to his heart she was so appreciative that he rewarded her with a small pension of 500 *écus* a year,

whereupon she hysterically embraced his knees and he was obliged to calm her down with kind words and further promises.

The *Princesse de Clèves,* an historical novel about the Court of Henri II, seems to have been conceived early in the year 1671. Many French critics think that, on the evidence of her letters to the Abbé Ménage and of her earlier novels, the *Princesse de Montpensier* and *Zayde,* which are really unreadable, Madame de Lafayette must have had a great deal of help with the *Princesse de Clèves;* some have definitely stated that it was by the Duc de la Rochefoucauld and others have attributed it to M. de Segrais. But it must be said in defense of Madame de Lafayette (and against this constantly recurring Bramwellism of the male critics) that it is by no means unheard of for an author to write a lot of very indifferent books and a single masterpiece. All writing depends for its merit upon the imaginative spark and upon the interest felt by the author in his subject; this spark and this interest could easily be lit by such a character as the Duc de Nemours or such a circumstance as Madame de Clèves' confession, and might not happen to be so lit again. However, speculation is useless and we shall never really know whether Madame de Lafayette wrote the *Princesse de Clèves* alone, or, if in collaboration, how much was hers and how much somebody's else. What we do know is that her little group of friends helped her enormously with the historical details, that they all settled down together to a minute study of Brantôme and the other historians and memorialists of Henri II and his

times, and that the novel was read and criticized and discussed, at every stage of its creation, in the *Chambre du Sublime.*

As a work of art the *Princesse de Clèves* stands alone. It needs no introduction. As a work of historical narrative it is as accurate as the information available when it was written could make it, and its author has quite recaptured the chivalrous and romantic attitude to love which prevailed in the Sixteenth Century—very different from the practical approach to her own generation. The relationship at Court, between royalty and commoners, the King and his mistress, the mistress and the other courtiers, and the various royal ladies among themselves were such as Madame de Lafayette had observed them at St. Cloud and Versailles, and these relationships probably had not changed very much in the course of a hundred years; nor had the manners and customs—for instance that of ladies receiving in their bedrooms, even lying on their beds. The hatred of the country, which made Madame de Clèves' longing to retire to it appear so suspicious to her husband, has always existed in the French nobility, and still does.

Indeed the whole book is intensely French, in its atmosphere, its point of view and in the virtues and vices of its characters; it could never have been produced by any other country. Especially so is the curious shrinking from happiness of Madame de Clèves herself, a state of mind that has been beautifully observed and recorded by Henry James in *The American* as well as, in a more extraverted way, by Balzac in the *Duchesse de Langeais,*

and which is to be found among Frenchwomen to this day. These three books all end on the same note, with the heroine escaping from life into a convent, but neither the boring American nor the rumbustious Général has the compelling fascination of M. de Nemours, a fascination so great that had Madame de Clèves' character been less perfectly understood and portrayed, it would be impossible to believe that she could have resisted him. It is Madame de Lafayette's final triumph that we can believe in the confession and can just believe in the renunciation.

All the characters in the book, except the Princess herself, Madame de Chartres and those of the story within a story about Madame de Tournon, are real people and all the anecdotes relating to Court life are quite true. The Duc de Nemours, perhaps the most irresistible character in any novel, was, as in the book, one of the champions of the fatal tournament. He was in love with the Duchesse de Guise. When the Duc de Guise died she refused at first to marry Nemours; in the end, however, unlike the Princesse de Clèves, she gave way and did marry him. Whether she subsequently suffered the fate which Madame de Clèves dreaded so terribly, of seeing him make love to other women, we do not know, but on the evidence of his character it is to be feared that she must have. The reader should not be put off by the long list of characters in the first pages of the book. It was a convention of the day to start a novel like that—they can very easily be skipped.

Hardly was the *Princesse de Clèves* begun than its progress was retarded by a terrible tragedy which befell M. de la Rochefoucauld. On one day, the 17th of June, 1671, in the war against Holland, his eldest son, the Prince de Marsillac, was gravely wounded, his second son, the Chevalier de Marsillac, was killed, and so was his adored illegitimate son, the Duc de Longueville, the idol of his old age. He was utterly broken by the death of M. de Longueville and could hardly even make the effort of pretending that his grief was on account of the Chevalier. His friends gave themselves up to trying to console him and surrounded him with love and attentions; a great deal of ingenuity had to be expended in keeping away *les pleureuses,* fashionable ladies like Mesdames de Brissac and de Marans who, each pretending to have been the beloved of M. de Longueville, would come and upset the poor Duke with their wailing. Not until December did he renew his interest in life; then, by degrees, his friends coaxed him to begin on a new set of Maxims and he soon turned his attention once more to the historical background for the *Princesse de Clèves*.

Another interruption occurred in February, 1673, when M. de Lafayette paid one of his rare visits to his family and bored them all to death with descriptions of beautiful nature in Auvergne. He seems to have enjoyed himself, and stayed on and on until at last the grape harvest made it necessary for him to go back. Hardly had he taken himself off than Madame de Sévigné returned to Paris after a long visit to Provence; she had to be wel-

comed, consoled for the parting with her daughter and told all the news. Then the Chevalier de Sévigné, Madame de Lafayette's step-father, died, leaving a tiresome will to be contested—another lawsuit. Then Segrais, that mine of historical information, decided to marry—most unnecessary of him—and as if that were not bad enough, to go to live at Caen. Finally, and far the most tedious of all, a thin sunburnt man appeared at the rue de Vaugirard announcing himself as M. de Lafayette's long-lost sailor brother, and proceeded to hold forth unceasingly about naval warfare and his two captured English frigates. Alas, every writer experiences this sort of interruptions and knows too well how upsetting they are to the quiet and even flow of thought without which creative work can hardly be achieved. To make things worse, Madame de Lafayette was now suffering in her liver and M. de la Rochefoucauld's gout was so bad that he often screamed aloud with pain; the only remedy that did him any good at all was viper soup, and the poor man longed for death.

At last, however, in 1677, the Princess was ready for her *début,* a ceremony that was prepared for months beforehand with the greatest care and attention to detail by Madame de Lafayette's little band of faithful admirers. Readings of the book were given to *"des personnes très éclairées"* who then did their bit by praising it to the skies wherever they went. Soon it was the talk of the town and everybody knew that it was by Madame de Lafayette, in spite of her strenuous disclaimers. In March, 1678, it appeared in the bookshops.

La
PRINCESSE
de
CLEVES
tôme I (II, III, IV)
à Paris
chez Claude Barbin au Palais
sur le second Perron de la Sainte
Chapelle
MDCLXX VIII
avec privilège du roi

This edition sold out immediately. An English translation was prepared: "The Princess of Clèves, the most famed romance written in French by the greatest Wits of France. Rendered into English by a Person of Quality."

It caused a sensation. The scene of the *aveu* provoked violent controversy as to the probability of any woman making such a confession to her husband; several long pamphlets were written abusing the book roundly, and were replied to at length by Madame de Lafayette and M. de la Rochefoucauld, who still pretended not to have the slightest idea who could have written it. In short, it was a great success, went from edition to edition, and is indisputably one of the classics of the French language.

The Duc de la Rochefoucauld was now very ill. He lingered on for two years after the publication of the *Princesse* and then became much worse, ran a high fever and took to his room. Madame de Lafayette, who could not go to his house to see him, took to her own room in

sympathy and here were brought alternating messages of hope and of hope abandoned. The case was put in the hands of the English doctor Talbot; under his treatment the fever abated and Madame de Sévigné thought he might effect a cure. The Duke, however, sent for Monseigneur Bossuet and received extreme unction; then, while the people round him were still praising the wonderful English remedy, he quietly died.

Madame de Lafayette was not the woman to repine for very long, and she had plenty of occupations to distract her. The lawsuits, more numerous and more complicated every year, took up much of her time; then she seems to have become a sort of agent or spy at the Court on behalf of Madame Royale, the Regent of Savoy, who, educated at the convent of Chaillot, had been one of her little friends there in the early days of married life. There were her two dreary sons to settle in their professions, the eldest, for whom she procured rich benefices, in the Church, and the second in the Army—the archives of the Ministère de la Guerre contain many letters from Madame de Lafayette on his behalf to Louvois; it does not seem to have crossed her mind that poor Louvois, running the whole war practically single-handed, might have other things to occupy his attention than getting young Lafayette out of scrapes and seeing that he was promoted. Young Lafayette was a boor, a bounder and a brute. When the time came for him to marry, his mother looked round for a suitable heiress and decided upon Mademoiselle de Lassay, but her father, the Marquis de Lassay, knowing the young man's reputation, was en-

tirely opposed to such a match. Madame de Lafayette was not at all discouraged. She proceeded to intrigue against him at Court and to blackmail him, even going as far as to have a *lettre de cachet* made out against him by one of her friends. When M. de Lassay at last found out who was at the bottom of all his troubles he went with the whole story to Madame de Maintenon, begging for her protection and saying, "May God defend all decent people against such a woman as Madame de Lafayette." In the end she found another heiress for her son, but they had no children and that branch of the family came to an end with him.

M. de Lafayette died unobtrusively soon after M. de la Rochefoucauld and this gave her still more work to do as, without, of course, ever going near them, she took over the administration of his properties.

Now that death and matrimony had deprived her of two of her more interesting friends, she resumed the old relationship with the Abbé Ménage. He was no longer what he had been since falling downstairs and so smashing his hip that it was what the French call "in crumbs," but no doubt he filled a gap; anyhow, she said that she now realized the value of such a friend. "How stupid are the young and what a price we have to pay for seeing things as they really are, the price of our youth."

Madame de Lafayette went on writing novels, but her characters never again came to life and the books are unreadable. At last she seems to have realized this herself; she gave up fiction and devoted her time to writing contemporary history in a *Mémoir de la Cour de France*

pour les années 1688 et 1689. This is an account of the Cologne electorate, the English revolution, the arrival in France of the English royal family in exile, and the Dutch war, all mixed up with gossip from the French royal residences and larded with comments, mostly unfavorable, upon the character and activities of Madame de Maintenon; it is written in an involved style very different from the limpid lucidity of the *Princesse de Clèves,* and was published in Amsterdam, 1731.

Madame de Lafayette's last years were not very agreeable; she was constantly racked with pain. "Some day you will all see why," she used to say, and indeed when an autopsy was made after her death it disclosed one kidney eaten away, the other purulent and containing a large stone, and two growths in the heart, the tip of which organ was all withered up and desiccated. She died in 1693, nursed to the end by faithful Madame de Sévigné, in the consolation of a religion which had played but little part in her life.

Nancy Mitford

THE PRINCESS OF CLEVES

THE last years of Henri II's reign saw a display of opulence and gallantry such as has never been equalled in France. The King himself, charming to look at, the very flower of his race, and a worthy successor to his father, François I, was a great lover of women. His passion for Diane de Poitiers, Duchesse de Valentinois, began when he was barely twenty, but was none the less violent for that, nor were the tokens she received of it any the less dazzling. He excelled at all forms of sport and much of his time was given up to it; every day there was tilting at the ring, hunting, tennis, ballets and the like. Madame de Valentinois' colors and cyphers were very much in evidence, and so was she herself, dressed in a style which would have been more suitable for Mlle. de la Marck, her own grand-daughter, who was then just growing up. The presence of the Queen was her warrant. Catherine de Medicis though no longer in her first youth, was still a beautiful woman; the King had married her when he was Duc d'Orléans before the death of his elder brother the Dauphin.

She loved pomp, circumstance and pleasure, and, since she was ambitious, took great delight in reigning; she hardly seemed to mind the King's attachment to the Duchesse de Valentinois and she gave no sign of jealousy, but then she was a mistress of pretense, her real thoughts never easy to guess. In any case, it was expedient for her

to keep the Duchess closely attached to her person, since this also insured the presence of the King.

The King liked to be surrounded by women even when he was not in love with them, and every day he went to the Queen's apartments at the hour when she was at home, knowing he would find all that was most beautiful and elegant of both sexes. So many lovely women and handsome men have never been gathered together at one court; it seemed as if nature herself had taken a particular delight in bestowing her most coveted prizes upon the most exalted personages.

Madame Elizabeth of France, who became Queen of Spain, already showed signs of exceptional intelligence and of that beauty which was to prove so fatal to her happiness. Marie Stuart, the Queen of Scotland, who had just married the Dauphin, and whom they called the Queen-Dauphine, was perfection, both in mind and body. She was brought up at the Court of France, had assimilated all its elegance, and was born with so great a love of beauty that, in spite of her youth she knew and understood more about art than anybody. The Queen, her mother-in-law, and Madame, the King's sister, also loved poetry, drama and music; François I had made such things the fashion, the taste for them remained, and, since the King, his son, was so fond of outdoor amusements, it can be said that every form of pleasure was to be found at his Court. But its special radiance and magnificence came from the number of princes and great nobles, who, in different ways, adorned their generation.

The King of Navarre was universally respected, both

for his rank and for his lofty character. He was a first rate soldier. The Duc de Guise was his rival; indeed he often left his post as General to go to fight in the thick of the battle like a private soldier, side by side with the Duke. This Duke was so brave and successful that the greatest captains of his time felt an admiration not unmixed with envy for him; his courage was only one of many great qualities, since he combined intellect with a noble character and a practical capacity both for war and for politics. The Cardinal of Lorraine, his brother, was overweeningly ambitious, witty, eloquent and learned; at a time when many new attacks were being launched on the Roman Catholic Church, he used his learning in her defense, which added to his own prestige. Another brother, the Chevalier de Guise, later known as the Grand Prior, was a prince whom everybody loved —handsome, witty, clever, and famous throughout Europe for his great courage. The Prince de Condé had an indomitable soul in his small crooked body, and was so amusing that the most beautiful women fell in love with him. The Duc de Nevers, in spite of his advanced age, was an ornament of the Court, and had covered himself with glory both in warfare and in the various high offices which he had held during his lifetime. Of his three handsome sons, the second, known as the Prince de Clèves, had all the qualities necessary to uphold the luster of his name; he was brave, generous, and prudent beyond his years. The Vidame de Chartres was descended from the ancient house of Vendôme, a name famous in love and war which even Princes of the Blood

have not been too proud to bear. He was brave and handsome, generous and lively; these qualities were self-evident, and if any human being could be said to be worthy of comparison with the Duc de Nemours, it might be he.

But Nemours was a masterpiece. Not only was he the best looking and the bravest of men, but he had a mental distinction and charm that informed his whole aspect, setting him apart from his fellows. Both men and women found him fascinating; he excelled at sport, and his clothes and the way he wore them set the fashion but were inimitable—in short there was something about his personality which made it impossible to look at anybody else when he was there. There was not a lady at that Court whose reputation would not have been enhanced had he been in love with her. Very few of those to whom he paid attentions could boast of having resisted him; indeed several had loved him without any evidence that they were loved in return. He had such a sweet and affectionate nature, and was so ready to love that he could never harden his heart against anybody who tried to please him; the result was that he had several mistresses and it would have been difficult to guess which of them he really cared for. He was often to be found in the company of the Queen-Dauphine, and some people thought that he even lifted his eyes to her, which was not impossible, considering the beauty and sweetness of this lady, her infinite desire to please and the particular favor she always showed the Duke.

Her uncles, the Guise brothers, had risen in the world

by her marriage, and now their ambition was equality with the Princes of the Blood. They also wanted power, the sort of power that was wielded by the Connétable de Montmorency, to whom the King left most of the business of government, the Duc de Guise and the Maréchal de Saint André being merely treated as favorite companions. But whether the King was drawn to people by affection or by interest they could only maintain their position by deferring to the Duchesse de Valentinois because, though she now had neither youth nor beauty left, she governed the King so completely that she could be said to be mistress both of his person and of the whole realm.

The King had always loved the Constable, and as soon as he succeeded to the throne he recalled him from the exile to which François I had condemned him.

The courtiers were divided: some were for the Guises, and some, among whom were the Princes of the Blood, supported the Constable, and each side was anxious to get the support of the Duchesse de Valentinois. The Duc d'Aumale, brother of the Duc de Guise, had married one of her daughters, and the Constable wanted a similar relationship. It was not enough for him that he had married his eldest son to Diane, daughter of the King by a Piedmontese lady who had gone into a convent as soon as the child was born. The marriage had not been easy to arrange because M. de Montmorency had become involved with a Mademoiselle de Piennes, one of the Queen's ladies, and although the King had arranged matters with the greatest tact and kindness the Constable

still felt that he was not quite secure while Madame de Valentinois was so close to the Duc de Guise.

Now this lady herself was beginning to feel uneasy over the Duke's great ascendancy. She had held up the Queen of Scots' marriage to the Dauphin for as long as possible. The beauty and precocious intelligence of this young Queen, and the prestige which her marriage brought to the Guise family, were almost more than she could bear. She particularly disliked the Cardinal de Lorraine, who was sarcastic, condescending even, in his attitude towards her, and appeared to be taking the Queen's side. So the Constable found her well disposed towards him and ready to make an alliance by marrying Mlle. de la Marck, her grand-daughter, to his second son, M. d'Anville (who, later on, in the reign of Charles IX, was to succeed to his office). It never occurred to the Constable that M. d'Anville might be difficult over this marriage as his brother had been over his, but nevertheless such was the case, though the real reason for it was not disclosed. M. d'Anville was hopelessly in love with the Queen-Dauphine and, though he could expect little enough of this passion, he could not bear to enter upon an engagement which would oblige him to pay attentions to somebody else as well.

The only courtier who had not taken sides was the Maréchal de Saint André. The King had loved him ever since he was Dauphin, and had made him a Marshal of France at an age when it is most unusual to receive any honors at all. This gave M. de Saint André a prestige which he kept by virtue of his own superiority and

charm, the excellence of his table, the taste with which his house was arranged, and by a liberality such as few private people can afford—all made possible by the King's generosity. The King was prodigal with those he loved; though by no means perfect he had many qualities. He was a born soldier, experienced and successful in war; except for the Battle of Saint Quentin his reign was one victory after another. He had won, in person, the battle of Renti, had conquered Piedmont, driven the English from France, and turned the luck of the Emperor Charles V before his very own eyes outside the town of Metz when he was vainly besieging it with all the forces of the Empire and of Spain. Nevertheless the disaster at Saint Quentin had lowered our hopes of victory, and since the fortunes of war now seemed to be divided between the two Kings, their thoughts turned to peace.

The dowager Duchesse de Lorraine had begun to make overtures at the time of the Dauphin's wedding, and ever since then some secret negotiations or other had been carried on. Finally, Cercamp, in the Artois country, was chosen as a meeting place. The Cardinal de Lorraine, the Connétable de Montmorency and the Maréchal de Saint André represented the King; the Duke of Alba and the Prince of Orange were there for Philip II, while the Duc and Duchesse de Lorraine acted as mediators. The principal clauses referred to the marriage of Madame Elizabeth of France with Don Carlos, Infante of Spain, and of Madame, the King's sister, with the Duke of Savoy.

Nevertheless the King did not leave the frontier, and it

9

was here that he heard of the death of Mary Tudor. He sent the Comte de Randan to congratulate Elizabeth upon her succession, and she received him gladly since her rights were not too well established, and it was an advantage to be recognized by the King. The Count discovered that she was well informed about the French Court, its personalities and their various merits, and that in particular she knew all about the Duc de Nemours. She spoke to him so often and so earnestly of the Duke that when M. de Randan on his return was giving the King an account of his journey he mentioned the fact that, in his opinion, M. de Nemours could do anything he liked with the Queen, even to marrying her. The King spoke to the Duke about it that very evening, making M. de Randan repeat all the conversations he had had with Elizabeth, and advised him to go and see if he could not win this tremendous prize. At first M. de Nemours hardly believed that the King was serious, but when he saw that he was:

At least sire, he said, if I do set forth on so extravagant a venture, encouraged by your Majesty and to serve you, I must ask that it may be kept a secret until I have been justified by success, or it will appear that my vanity is such as to make me imagine that a Queen, who has never even set eyes on me, could wish to marry me.

The King agreed. He said he would only speak of their plan to the Constable, and in fact he considered that secrecy was an essential of success. M. de Randan advised the Duc de Nemours to go to England as an ordinary traveller, but the Duke could not bring himself

to do that. He sent Lignerolle, a clever young man and a favorite of his, to try to establish a relationship with the Queen and to sound her as to her real feelings, and while awaiting the results of this journey he went to Brussels to visit the Duke of Savoy, who was there with the King of Spain. Various difficulties having arisen out of Mary of England's death, the conference broke up at the end of November, and the King returned to Paris.

Now there appeared at the Court a beauty. All eyes were upon her and she must indeed have been a paragon to be so much admired in a place where lovely women were the rule. She belonged to the same family as the Vidame de Chartres, and was one of the greatest heiresses in France. Her father had died young, leaving her to be brought up by his widow, Madame de Chartres, a good, noble, and distinguished person. For some years after her husband's death she left the Court and devoted herself to her daughter's education, not only cultivating her mind and caring for her beauty, but also trying to make her good and give her a real love of virtue. Most mothers think that they can best protect their children by never speaking of love in their presence, but Madame de Chartres had different ideas; she often described it to her daughter, minimizing none of its charm so that the girl should more readily understand what she told her of its dangers. She told her that men were not very sincere, not very faithful and not above deceit; she spoke of the unhappiness that love affairs can bring to a family, and then, on the other hand, she showed her

the life of a good woman—happy, serene, and enjoying the particular glamor that attaches to noble birth when there is also virtue. She impressed upon her that this virtue can only be kept by vigilance and by following the one line of conduct which can make a woman happy —that is to say, loving her husband and being loved by him.

The girl was such an heiress that, though still extremely young, she had already received several proposals of marriage, but Madame de Chartres, who was as proud as Lucifer, could hardly conceive of anything grand enough for her daughter, and decided, when she was in her sixteenth year, to take her to Court. As soon as she arrived the Vidame called to see her; he was astonished, as well he might be, at the beauty of Mademoiselle de Chartres. She was absolutely dazzling, indeed there was nobody to touch her, with her white skin, golden hair, classical features, and general aspect of sweetness and charm.

The day after her arrival she went to match some precious stones at the house of an Italian who did a worldwide traffic in such things. This man had come from Florence with the Queen and had waxed so rich that he lived more like a great noble than a merchant. While she was there the Prince de Clèves arrived. His astonishment at her beauty was undisguised, so much so that Mademoiselle de Chartres, seeing the state into which she had thrown him, could not help blushing. She regained her composure, however, and paid no more attention to the Prince and his behavior than was demanded

by ordinary politeness to a man of quality. M. de Clèves gazed at her with admiration, unable to imagine who such a beautiful person, evidently, from her manner and her attendants, of the highest rank, and yet unknown to him, could possibly be. As she was so young he thought that she was probably unmarried, but she had no mother with her, while the Italian, who did not know her, called her Madame; he was completely puzzled. He continued to stare, but he noticed that, whereas most young people enjoy seeing the effects of their beauty upon others, it only embarrassed her, and he felt that he was hastening her departure. Indeed, very soon she left. M. de Clèves consoled himself by the thought that now he would find out who she was, but, greatly to his surprise, nobody could tell him. An impression of beauty and purity remained with him; he seems then and there to have conceived an overwhelming esteem for her and to have fallen in love.

That evening he went to see Madame, the King's sister, a Princess who was universally respected on account of the high credit in which she stood with the King, her brother—so high, indeed, that when making peace the King had consented to give up his claim to Piedmont so that she could marry the Duke of Savoy. All her life she had wished to be married, but she would not take any but a sovereign, and for this reason had refused the King of Navarre when he was the Duc de Vendôme. She had hoped to marry the Duke of Savoy, ever since seeing him at Nice during the meeting there between King François I and Pope Paul III. She was a clever

woman with a great love of art; she attracted distinguished people to her, and at certain hours of the day the whole Court could be found in her rooms. M. de Clèves went there as usual, so full of the charm and beauty of Mademoiselle de Chartres that he could speak of nothing else, telling his adventure to all and sundry and singing the praises of this mysterious lady. Madame told him that no such person existed because if she did they would all know her, but Madame de Dampierre, her lady-in-waiting, who was a friend of Madame de Chartres, overheard the conversation, and she whispered to the Princess that it must have been Mademoiselle de Chartres whom the Prince de Clèves had seen. So Madame turned to him and said that if he came the following day she would arrange for him to meet his beauty.

Accordingly, the next day Mademoiselle de Chartres made her first appearance. She was received with the greatest kindness by the two Queens, and with such admiration by everybody else, that she heard nothing but praise on every hand. This she accepted quite simply as though she hardly noticed it, and it affected her behavior not at all. Next she went to Madame, the King's sister, who complimented her on her beauty and then told her of the bewilderment into which she had thrown M. de Clèves. A moment later the Prince himself appeared.

Come in, she said. Now, have I not kept my word? In showing you Mademoiselle de Chartres am I not showing the very beauty whom you were seeking? And now

you may thank me, for I have already told her how much you admire her.

M. de Clèves was overjoyed to find that this lady, who had seemed to him made for love, was as well-born as she was beautiful. He went over to her and begged her never to forget the regard he had felt for her before he even knew her name. He and his friend the Chevalier de Guise then went off together, singing the praises of Mademoiselle de Chartres. At last they felt that they must be exaggerating and fell silent, keeping their thoughts to themselves. All the same, whenever they met during the days that followed it was of her that they talked, and, indeed, this new beauty was for a long time the chief subject of every conversation. The Queen was full of her praises and was unusually good to her; the Queen-Dauphine made a favorite of her and begged Madame de Chartres to bring her often. The King's daughters sent for her to join in all their games. In fact the whole Court loved her and thought her beautiful; the one exception was Madame de Valentinois—not because she thought that the new beauty would put her in the shade, since by long experience she knew quite well that as far as the King was concerned she had nothing to fear, but because she was on very bad terms with the Vidame de Chartres. She had hoped to get him on her side through the marriage of one of his daughters, but he had preferred to be of the Queen's party. She could not therefore feel favorably disposed towards a lady of his name and whom he evidently loved very much.

The Prince de Clèves, now deeply in love with Made-

moiselle de Chartres, longed to marry her, but he was afraid that Madame de Chartres would be too proud to give her daughter to any but the head of a house. Nevertheless his family was so important (the head of it, the Comte d'Eu, having recently married a lady nearly connected with the Royal Family) that his fears were hardly reasonable, but came from the natural diffidence of a man in love. He had many rivals; the most dangerous seemed to be the Chevalier de Guise on account of his birth, his qualities, and the royal favor which his family enjoyed.

This Prince had fallen in love with Mademoiselle de Chartres the very first day he saw her. He and M. de Clèves were fully aware of each other's feelings for the lady, their rivalry causing a coolness between them so that they were never able to discuss the matter frankly. M. de Clèves felt it a good omen that he should have been the first to see her—it seemed to give him a start on his rivals—but he foresaw that his father, the Duc de Nevers, would make difficulties. The Duke was hand in glove with Madame de Valentinois, and, since she was at war with the Vidame de Chartres, he was not very likely to allow his son to think of the Vidame's niece.

It may be imagined that Madame de Chartres, who had been at such pains to instil virtue into her daughter's character, did not relax her precautions in a place so full of bad examples, and indeed they had never been so necessary. The Court gravitated round ambition and love, the chief occupations of men and women alike, for

there were so many factions and intrigues, and the women played so large a part in them, that love and politics were inseparable. Tranquillity, indifference, boredom and idleness, were unknown; everybody was busily trying to better their position by pleasing, by helping or by hindering somebody else. The occupations of the day were pleasure and plots. The women attached themselves to the Queen, the Queen-Dauphine, the Queen of Navarre, Madame, the King's sister, or the Duchesse de Valentinois, according to inclination, interest, or whim. Those past their first youth, or who professed a certain puritanism, were in the Queen's set. Younger ones, in pursuit of love and happiness, courted the Queen-Dauphine. The Queen of Navarre had her favorites; she was young and the King, her husband, listened to her. He was attached to the Constable, and this made him influential. Madame, the King's sister, still beautiful, attracted some of the women to her. The Duchesse de Valentinois could have anybody she liked, but she was not fond of women, and, with the exception of a very few intimate friends whose characters suited her, she only received them on those days when it amused her to hold a Court like the Queen's.

All these different cabals vied against each other incessantly, while at the same time the women who composed them had various jealousies among themselves, so that mixed up with the main objectives of place, promotion and love were many interests, of lesser importance certainly, but which were no less eagerly canvassed. The result was a discreetly exciting atmosphere which

made this Court an agreeable place to live in, though not without its dangers for the very young. Madame de Chartres was perfectly well aware of these dangers, and her great preoccupation was how best to guard her daughter against them. She begged her, not as a mother but rather as a friend, to confide in her whenever words of love were spoken, promising her guidance and support in those situations which can be so difficult for the young.

The Chevalier de Guise made no secret of his feelings and wishes with regard to Mademoiselle de Chartres; everybody knew of them, but look at it which way he would he saw that what he so much desired was hardly possible. He knew that he was not a suitable husband for Mademoiselle de Chartres, since he had but little means to support his rank, and then his brothers would certainly oppose his marriage, fearing a reduction of power which the marriage of younger sons often brings to great families. The Cardinal de Lorraine, for his part, soon let him see that he was not mistaken, warmly deploring his brother's inclination for Mademoiselle de Chartres, but without giving his real reasons. The Cardinal had a secret hatred for the Vidame which only exploded publicly later on, and he would have preferred any connection for his brother to one with this Vidame. He let it be seen so clearly how much he was opposed to the idea that Madame de Chartres was not a little offended, and was at great pains to put it about that the Cardinal had nothing to fear since she would not even consider this marriage. The Vidame did likewise. He was even more annoyed by

the Cardinal's behavior than Madame de Chartres, since he had a better idea of what caused it.

The Prince de Clèves, unlike the Chevalier de Guise, had not made his feelings public, and it was with dismay that the Duc de Nevers learnt of them; nevertheless he supposed that he would only have to have a word with his son to make him change his mind. He was very much surprised and very disapproving when he found that the Prince was perfectly decided upon marrying Mademoiselle de Chartres. He fell into a rage which he was at so little pains to conceal that the whole Court, including Madame de Chartres, soon knew exactly what was going on. It had not even occurred to her that M. de Nevers could regard his son's marriage with her daughter otherwise than as a great privilege, and she was disagreeably surprised to find that the houses of Clèves and Guise, instead of wishing for the connection, should seem to fear it. Such was her indignation that she now had a mind to marry her daughter to somebody whose rank would put her above those who thought themselves too good for her. After some thought her choice fell upon the son of the Duc de Montpensier, who was just grown up. Nobody at the Court was grander than he. Madame de Chartres was a clever person; she had the Vidame, with all his great prestige, to help her, and her daughter was a very considerable heiress. So well did she play her cards that M. de Montpensier was apparently in favor of the marriage and nothing seemed to stand in its way.

Now M. d'Anville was a close friend of the Prince de

Montpensier, and the Vidame had the idea of asking the Queen-Dauphine to get him on their side, which she could easily do as he was so deeply in love with her, and ask him to further the cause of Mademoiselle de Chartres with the King and the Prince de Montpensier. So he spoke about it to the Queen-Dauphine, who threw herself into the affair, since it was for the sake of Mademoiselle de Chartres whom she liked so much. She told the Vidame that she would be only too pleased to help, in spite of the fact that she would be crossing her uncle the Cardinal de Lorraine, a consideration that did not weigh too heavily with her as he was always taking the Queen's side against her.

Romantic young ladies are always glad of a pretext for talking with those they know are in love with them. As soon as the Vidame had taken his leave of the Queen-Dauphine she told Châtelart, M. d'Anville's friend, who knew of his love for her, to take him a message asking him to go that evening to the Queen's rooms. Châtelart respectfully and gladly undertook this commission. He was a gentleman from the Dauphiné, who, though his family was good, had made an even better place for himself by his own qualities and talents. All the great nobles of the Court accepted him and treated him kindly. He was specially attached to M. d'Anville through the patronage of the house of Montmorency. Handsome, good at all sport, he sang charmingly, wrote poetry, and had a passionately sentimental side to his character which so greatly pleased M. d'Anville that he had confided in him his love for the Queen-Dauphine. Alas, this con-

fidence was to prove fatal by bringing him within the orb of that lady; seeing her constantly he could not but fall in love, and this cost him his reason and eventually life itself.

M. d'Anville did not fail to go to the Queen that evening. He was only too happy to have been chosen by Madame la Dauphine to help with something she wanted, and he promised her that he would do exactly as she said. But Madame de Valentinois, having been warned that this marriage was in the air, had taken so much trouble to prevent it, and had so put the King against it, that when M. d'Anville spoke to him he gave him clearly to understand that it would have no support from him, and even commanded him to say so to the Prince de Montpensier.

Madame de Chartres' feelings may be imagined. Not only had her plan failed, but, by its failure, had put her enemies in a better position, while damaging the prospects of her child. The Queen-Dauphine told Mademoiselle de Chartres in a most friendly way that she was very sorry not to have been more helpful.

You see, she said, my power here is but limited. The Queen and Madame de Valentinois both hate me so much that they always manage to prevent me getting my own way, either directly or through their followers. And I have tried so hard to make them like me. They hate me because years ago they were jealous and suspicious of the Queen my mother. The King was in love with her before he was with Madame de Valentinois, and then during the first childless years of his marriage,

he seemed to be thinking of a divorce in order to marry the Queen my mother, although he now loved Madame de Valentinois. She, terrified lest he should marry a woman he had already loved and who was quite beautiful and clever enough to put her in the shade, joined forces with the Constable, who, on his side, was not at all happy at the idea that the King might marry a sister of the Guises. They got the late King on their side, in spite of his deadly hatred for Madame de Valentinois, by playing on his love for the Queen his daughter-in-law and made him work with them against a divorce. In order to get my mother out of the way they married her to the King of Scotland, widower of the King's sister Madame Magdeleine, choosing him because it could be done at once. Thus they broke faith with the King of England with whom there had been an understanding and who greatly wished to marry her. Indeed this nearly caused a quarrel between the two Kings. Henry VIII never got over not having married my mother, and whenever French princesses were offered to him he always said they were no substitute for the one of whom he had been cheated. My mother certainly was a great beauty, and it is a remarkable thing that no fewer than three sovereigns should have wanted to marry the widow of a Duc de Longueville. To her misfortune she married the least important of them, and found herself in a country where there was nothing but trouble. I often wonder whether I shall be any luckier than she was, in spite of the apparent happiness of my lot.

Mademoiselle de Chartres told the Queen that these

were sad and unlikely presentiments and begged her not to doubt but that her future would be all it seemed.

After this, none of the men dared to think of marrying Mademoiselle de Chartres. Some feared that by doing so they would annoy the King, and others felt that they were not grand enough for somebody who had hoped for a Prince of the Blood. M. de Clèves alone was influenced by neither of these considerations. The death of his father, the Duc de Nevers, which occurred at this time, left him perfectly free to do as he liked, and as soon as his mourning was over he had but one idea, how best to arrange his marriage with Mademoiselle de Chartres. He thought himself in luck since, at the very time when he wanted to propose, these things had happened to frighten away the other suitors and make it more likely that he would be accepted. His happiness would have been complete had he felt sure of her love, since it was her love he wanted, far more than the certainty of marrying her without it. He had been rather jealous of the Chevalier de Guise, but this jealousy was founded less upon anything he could notice in Mademoiselle de Chartres' manner than upon the qualities of the Prince himself. He longed to know how matters stood for him, and whether she smiled upon his suit, but how to find out? He never saw her except with the two Queens, or at receptions, and it was very difficult to speak with her alone. However he did succeed in doing so, and then, with deep respect he told her of his love and his hopes for the future, begging her to say what her feelings were for him. He added that he did not want

her to accept him simply in order to please her mother, or from a sense of duty, but that, on the contrary, his feelings for her were such that this could only bring unhappiness.

Since Mademoiselle de Chartres had a charming nature she was touched to the heart, and in her gratitude for M. de Clèves' behavior she answered with a sort of sweetness which was quite enough to raise the hopes of a man so desperately in love, and he began to think that very likely everything was as he wished.

She reported the conversation to her mother, who told her that she would gladly consent if Mademoiselle de Chartres felt inclined to marry him, enlarging upon his many qualities, noble character, and wisdom beyond his years. Mademoiselle de Chartres replied that she knew he was good, that she would indeed marry him with less reluctance than another, but that she was not particularly attracted by his person. The next day proposals on behalf of the Prince were made to Madame de Chartres and she accepted them. She felt no qualms; it never even occurred to her that she was perhaps giving her daughter to somebody whom she could not love. The contract was drawn up, the King was informed, and the engagement was then announced.

M. de Clèves was happy without feeling quite satisfied. Mademoiselle de Chartres was grateful to him and had a good opinion of him, but he saw to his sorrow that that was all, and did not flatter himself that there were any hidden depths, because if there had been, even her extreme modesty would not, in their present situation,

have forbidden her to reveal them. So hardly a day passed but he complained bitterly to her.

How can I not be happy now that I am to marry you? Yet truly I am not. You only have a sort of kindness for me which cannot satisfy me; you have no fever, no longing, none of the agonies of love. In fact I might be marrying you not for yourself but for your money, and my terrible passion seems to pass by you unnoticed.

You are not being fair to me, she replied. What more can you want? I think it would hardly be seemly for me to go any further than I do.

He said, I would be quite contented with your attitude if only I could feel that there was something more, but as for seemliness holding you back I always have the impression that it alone forces you to go as far as you do. I have failed to touch your heart, and my presence neither pleases nor disturbs you.

How can you, she said, think that it gives me no pleasure to be with you? As for disturbance, surely you must have noticed how often I blush at the sight of you?

I am not taken in by your blushes, he said. They are simply a sign of modesty and have nothing to do with love. I only take such satisfaction from them as I may.

All these shades of sentiment being above her head Mademoiselle de Chartres had no idea what answer she ought to make; M. de Clèves saw only too well that she could not possibly have the feelings he so longed for her to have since she did not even understand what they were.

The Chevalier de Guise, who had been away, returned

a few days before the wedding. Though he had given up all hope of marrying Mademoiselle de Chartres, the difficulties seeming too great, he felt none the less very sad when he saw her about to marry another, and this grief by no means extinguished his passion. He was as much in love as ever. Mademoiselle de Chartres had been in no doubt as to the feelings of the Prince for her. Now that he was back again he gave her to understand that she was the cause of his sad looks; he was so good and so charming that she could not but feel compassion for him, especially as she was responsible for his wretchedness. So she pitied him, but this pity did not lead to any other feelings and she confided it to her mother.

Madame de Chartres admired her daughter's candor, as well she might. Nobody ever had a more frank and open nature, and not least did she admire the fact that her heart had remained untouched, especially as she knew quite well that neither the Prince de Clèves nor anybody else had ever touched it. She took all the more trouble to make her love her husband and to impress upon her how much she owed him for having fallen in love before he even knew who she was, a love to which he had borne witness by choosing her at a time when nobody else dared to think of her.

So this marriage took place. The ceremony was performed at the Louvre, and that evening the King, the Queens, and all the courtiers went to a splendid supper party given by Madame de Chartres. The Chevalier de Guise dared not make himself conspicuous by staying

away from this reception, but he could hardly conceal his misery.

M. de Clèves did not find that Mademoiselle de Chartres had changed her feelings with her name. As a husband he had new privileges but no new place in his wife's heart, so that, always longing for something out of his reach, he continued to behave like a lover, and though she was perfect in her behavior to him his passion for her was too violent and agitating for him to be happy. Jealousy did not enter into it; no wife ever gave less cause for that and no husband ever felt it less, in spite of the fact that she was exposed, at the Court, to every temptation. She went each day to the two Queens and to Madame; she met all the young and attractive men in her own rooms and with her brother-in-law the Duc de Nevers, who kept open house, but she had a certain quality which imposed respect and made it impossible to flirt with her, so much so that even the Maréchal de Saint André, though he was nothing if not bold, and furthermore protected by the King's friendship, found himself moved by her beauty without daring to let this be seen. He was attentive but that was all. Several others were in the same case, and Madame de Chartres, by her own care for the proprieties combined with her daughter's goodness, managed to give the impression that here indeed was somebody quite out of reach.

The Duchesse de Lorraine, while working in the cause of peace, had also been busy making a match for her son the Duc de Lorraine. It was now settled, the bride being Madame Claude de France, the King's second daughter,

and the wedding was to take place in February. Now, all this while, the Duc de Nemours had been living at Brussels, perfectly absorbed by his English projects. He spent his time sending and receiving messengers, his hopes rose every day, and at last Lignerolle told him that the moment had come for him to go in person and conclude the matter which had begun so well. He was overjoyed at this news, as any young man would have been at seeing a crown within his grasp, simply on the strength of his own reputation. Though at first he had not believed in such a change of fortune he was now looking upon it as something normal and inevitable. He sent orders to Paris, by diligence, for a splendid retinue, that he might appear in England suitably equipped. Then he hastened to Paris himself for the wedding of M. de Lorraine. He arrived on the eve of the festivities and went at once to see the King to tell him what progress he had made so far and to ask for advice and instructions for the future. Then he called on the two Queens. Madame de Clèves did not happen to be there, so that she neither saw him nor knew of his arrival. She had heard so much of this Prince, as of the best looking, most charming man at the Court; Madame la Dauphine in particular was always talking about him, and in such a way as to have aroused her curiosity, so that she was quite impatient to see him.

There was to be a Court ball at the Louvre, and she spent the whole of that day in her own room getting ready for it. When she arrived she was greatly admired, for her clothes, her jewels and her beauty. The ball opened, and

while she was dancing with M. de Guise there was a stir at the entrance to the ballroom, people making way as though for somebody important. Madame de Clèves went on dancing, and while she was considering whom she should take for her next partner the King called to her to take the newcomer. She turned round and saw a man striding over benches to get to the dancing floor; at once she felt that this could be none other than M. de Nemours. The first sight of this handsome Prince, always quite startling, was made more so on this occasion by the trouble he had taken with his appearance, and equally the first sight of Madame de Clèves was an amazement. M. de Nemours was so much struck by her beauty that, as she curtseyed to him, he could not conceal his admiration. They began to dance together, and as they did so a murmur of applause ran round the ballroom. The King and Queens reminded each other that these two had never met before, and thought it strange to see them dancing without knowing each other. As soon as the dance was over they called them, giving them no opportunity to speak to anybody else, and asked if they were not dying of curiosity to know who the other was, or whether they had guessed.

For myself, said M. de Nemours, I am not in any doubt, but as Madame de Clèves has not the same reasons for knowing who I am as I had for recognizing her, I should be grateful if your Majesty would be good enough to tell her my name.

In my opinion, said the Dauphine, she knows it as well as you know hers.

Madame de Clèves, rather ill at ease, said, I assure you, Madame, that I am not as good at guessing as you seem to think.

You have guessed quite well, and it is very flattering to M. de Nemours, this refusal to admit that, though you have never seen him, nevertheless you know who he is.

The Queen now broke in, saying that the ball must go on, and M. de Nemours danced with the Queen-Dauphine. This lady had seemed to M. de Nemours perfectly beautiful (as indeed she was) before he went to Flanders, but now he had eyes for nobody but the Princesse de Clèves.

The Chevalier de Guise, who still worshipped her, sat at her feet, saddened by what he had just seen. It seemed inevitable, fore-ordained by fate itself, that M. de Nemours should fall in love with Madame de Clèves. Perhaps there was a shadow on her face, or perhaps the Chevalier, in his jealousy, sensed what was in fact more than the truth. Be that as it may, he thought her deeply affected by M. de Nemours, and could not help saying to her how lucky it was for the Prince to have begun their acquaintance in so strange and romantic a manner.

Madame de Clèves left the ball so greatly preoccupied by what had happened that, late as it was, she went to her mother's room to tell her about it, speaking of M. de Nemours in such terms that Madame de Chartres instantly had the same idea as the Chevalier de Guise.

Next day the wedding was solemnized and Madame de Clèves once more thought the charm and good looks of the Duc de Nemours quite extraordinary. During the

days which followed she saw him with the Dauphine, she saw him playing tennis with the King, she saw him tilting, and heard him talk. She saw that he was better at games than anybody, so witty and delightful that all conversation centered round him, and before long he had made a deep impression on her heart. Since M. de Nemours for his part felt violently attracted to her and behaved with that slightly fantastic sweetness which often, at first, accompanies a great desire to please, he was even more fascinating than usual. Thus seeing each other all the time, and seeing in each other the very best elements of that Court, they could not but be charmed by what they saw.

The Duchesse de Valentinois was at all the parties, the King showing the same lively affection and paying her the same attentions as when he was first in love. Madame de Clèves, who was at an age when it seems impossible that any woman over twenty-five could be loved, was astonished to see the King's devotion for this grandmother, whose grand-daughter had just married. She spoke of this to Madame de Chartres.

How is it possible, she said, that the King can have been in love for so long and how can he have formed this attachment in the first place for a woman, much older than he, who was his father's mistress and who still, from what one hears, has many lovers?

Her mother replied, It is not certainly for her merit. I must say that if she had been different, as young, beautiful, and virtuous, for instance, as she was well born, had she loved only the King and loved him for himself alone

31

and not for what he could give her, and had she used her influence for his own good, it would have been impossible not to admire such constancy on his part. If I did not fear that you would say, as people always do of women when they get to be my age, that they tell nothing but old stories of the past, I would tell you how it happened that the King fell in love with this duchess, and many details about the late King's Court besides, which are not unrelated to the present.

If I had a complaint, said the Princess, it would be that you never tell me enough, either about the past or the present. I am so ignorant of the various interests and combinations around me that only a few days ago I still thought the Constable and the Queen were friends.

Yes indeed, that is very far from being the case, replied Madame de Chartres. The Queen hates M. le Connétable, and if ever she gets any power into her hands he will be made to feel it. She knows quite well he is forever telling the King that the only ones of his children who look the least bit like him are the bastards.

How could I possibly guess at this hatred, interrupted Madame de Clèves, when it is well known that the Queen wrote to M. le Connétable while he was in prison, and seemed overjoyed at his release? Besides which, she, as well as the King, always calls him Godfather.

If you judge by appearances in this place, replied Madame de Chartres, you will go on making mistakes, for things here are seldom what they seem. But to go back to Madame de Valentinois, you know of course that her real name is Diane de Poitiers and that she comes of an

illustrious house, descending from the Dukes of Aquitaine. One of her forbears was an illegitimate daughter of Louis XI—in short, there is nothing mediocre about her birth. Saint Vallier, her father, became involved in the affair of the Connétable de Bourbon which you mentioned just now, and was condemned to be executed, and even led to the scaffold. But his daughter, who was remarkably beautiful and was already in favor with the late King, succeeded, how I do not know, in obtaining the life of her father. They took his reprieve to him when he had ceased to expect anything but the fatal blow, but he was so terror-struck that he died a few days later. The daughter then appeared at Court as the King's mistress, but the affair was interrupted by his journey to Italy and his imprisonment. On his return from Spain, his mother, the regent, came to Bayonne to meet him, bringing all her ladies, including a Mademoiselle de Pisselieu, who has since become Duchesse d'Etampes, and with her the King fell in love. She was neither as well born, as witty, nor as beautiful as Madame de Valentinois, and in fact had only one advantage over her, that of extreme youth. I have heard it said that she was born on the very day that Diane de Poitiers was married, but I think this is a spiteful invention because, if I am not mistaken, the Duchesse de Valentinois married M. de Bréze, High Seneschal of Normandy, just about the time when the King was falling in love with Madame d'Etampes. There could be no greater hatred than existed between these two women. The Duchesse de Valentinois never forgave Madame d'Etampes for stealing the title of

King's mistress, and Madame d'Etampes was violently jealous of the other because the King never quite dropped her. It was not the habit of this Prince to be faithful to one mistress at a time. He used to have one who enjoyed the title and honors of the position, but his attentions were taken in turn by ladies of what was called the "little set."

It was a terrible blow to the King when his eldest son died at Tournon of suspected poisoning. He was not nearly so fond of his second son, our present King, whom he thought much less of a personality, and he complained about him to the Duchesse de Valentinois. She said that she would make him fall in love with her—that this would liven him up and make him more attractive. As you know, she succeeded perfectly and this love has now lasted, unshaken by the passing of time or anything else at all, for twenty long years. The King was against it from the first. He may still have been fond enough of Madame de Valentinois to be jealous, or perhaps the Duchesse d'Etampes, in despair at seeing the Dauphin under the influence of her rival, may have worked on his feelings; in any case he was angry and unhappy about it and made no secret of the fact. However, he did not succeed in intimidating his son, who went on steadily and quite openly with the love affair, so that in the end the King was obliged to put up with it, though it made a breach between him and the Dauphin. The result was that he turned to his third son, the Duc d'Orléans, a handsome, graceful, rather harum-scarum boy, full of fire and ambition, who needed a strong hand but

who would have made a first-class prince if he had lived long enough to have been ripened by age. The two brothers had been rivals from the nursery, and now that the Dauphin enjoyed the privileges of an eldest son, while the Duc d'Orléans was his father's favorite, their rivalry turned to hatred. When the Emperor was in France he put the Duc d'Orléans before the Dauphin, who resented it so bitterly that at Chantilly, where the Emperor was, he tried to force the Connétable de Bourbon to put a stop to it without waiting for orders from the King. The Constable refused, and afterwards found himself blamed by the King for not having listened to his son, and all this had a great deal to do with his leaving the Court.

Seeing the brothers so much estranged, Madame d'Etampes had the idea of getting the Duc d'Orléans on her side against Madame de Valentinois. She succeeded, and although the Prince was not in love with her he worked almost as much for her interests as the Dauphin did for those of Madame de Valentinois. So you see there were two factions at Court, intriguing away, and not only over the squabbles of women. The Emperor, who remained friendly with M. d'Orléans, more than once offered him the Duchy of Milan, and while proposals for peace were being considered he allowed him to hope for the Seventeen Provinces and the hand of his daughter. The Dauphin wished neither for peace nor for this marriage and he made the Constable, whom he had always liked, put it to the King that it would be most unwise to saddle his successor with a brother as powerful as the

Duc d'Orléans would become, if related by marriage to the Emperor, and with the Seventeen Provinces at his back. The Constable agreed with the Dauphin, all the more so because, in this, he was working against his open enemy Madame d'Etampes, who, of course, greatly wished for this aggrandizement of the Duc d'Orléans.

Now the Dauphin was in command of the King's army in Champagne and had so reduced the Imperial forces that they would have been wiped out had not the Duchesse d'Etampes, fearing that, if this happened, we should refuse both to make peace and to allow the Duc d'Orléans' alliance with the Emperor, secretly sent word to the enemy that he would do well to take Epernay and Château Thierry, both of which were filled with provisions. He did so, and by this means saved his army. The Duchess did not enjoy the fruits of her treachery for long; very soon the Duc d'Orléans died from some sort of contagion at Farmontier. He had been in love with one of the most beautiful women at the Court and was loved by her in return. I am not going to tell you her name. She has led a good life ever since, and has been at such pains to conceal the love she had for the Prince that she deserves to keep her reputation. It so happened that she received news of her husband's death on the same day as that of the Duke, so that she was not obliged to act a part or to conceal her sorrow.

The King only survived his son by two years. He had strongly recommended to the Dauphin that he should take the Cardinal de Tournon and Admiral d'Annebault as his advisers, saying nothing about the Constable, who

had been banished to his estates at Chantilly. The first action of the new King, however, was to send for him and put him at the head of the government. Madame d'Etampes was sent away, and was as badly treated as she could have expected to be by an all-powerful enemy. The Duchesse de Valentinois revenged herself to the full, not only on Madame d'Etampes, but on all the people who had earned her displeasure. Her influence over the King was unchallenged, even more complete than it had been when he was Dauphin, and so it is now that he has reigned these twelve years. It is she who makes appointments and disposes of offices. She dismissed the Cardinal de Tournon, Chancelier Olivier and Ville-roy, and whenever anybody has been rash enough to have tried opening the King's eyes to her real conduct they have lost everything as a result. The Comte de Taix, Grandmaster of the Artillery, who did not like her at all, could not resist talking about her love affairs, and es-pecially of that with the Comte de Brissac, of whom the King was already jealous; she managed so well that the Comte de Taix was disgraced, exiled, and relieved of his position. Unbelievable as it may seem, this was then bestowed upon Brissac, who was presently made Marshal of France through the efforts of the Duchess. The King's jealousy, however, got so much worse that he could not bear to see the Marshal at Court. Now jealousy, such a bitter and violent emotion with most people, always affects him very mildly because of the awe in which he stands of his mistress, and in this case he dared not exile his rival on some pretext, but made him Governor of

Piedmont. M. de Brissac stayed there for several years, coming back last winter, ostensibly to ask for more soldiers and for various things needed by the armies under his command, but perhaps really because he longed to see Madame de Valentinois again, fearing that otherwise she might forget all about him. He was coldly received by the King. The Guises, who hate him but dare not show it because of Madame de Valentinois, used her declared enemy the Vidame to prevent Brissac from obtaining any of the things he wanted. It was not at all difficult to put a spoke in his wheel; the King hated him so much and felt so uneasy in his presence that he was obliged to go away again without anything to show for his journey, unless it was that he had rekindled a spark in Madame de Valentinois' heart which absence had begun to extinguish. This is not the only grounds for jealousy which the King has had, but either he had not known about the others or else he has never dared to complain of them.

Madame de Chartres then added, Perhaps you think it quite unnecessary for me to have told you all this.

That, replied Madame de Clèves, is the last complaint I am likely to make, and now that I know you are ready to tell I shall often be asking you to explain things I do not understand.

M. DE NEMOURS' love for Madame de Clèves was so violent in its first stages that he could take no interest in the other women he used to love, with some of whom he had kept in touch while he was away. Indeed he quite forgot all about them. He seized every opportunity to break with them and could not bring himself to listen to their complaints or answer their reproaches. The Dauphine, with whom formerly he had been rather in love, had no chance against Madame de Clèves, and even his impatience for the English journey began to cool—he was not pressing forward his plans with any of his former enthusiasm.

He saw a good deal of the Queen-Dauphine because Madame de Clèves was constantly there; besides, it suited him perfectly that people should go on thinking he was in love with the Dauphine. He set Madame de Clèves on such a pedestal that he resolved rather to give too few indications of his love than to risk it being made public. He did not even speak of it to his great friend the Vidame de Chartres, from whom he never as a rule kept anything. Altogether he behaved very sensibly, so that few people had any idea he might be in love with Madame de Clèves; she herself would hardly have been aware of it had her own inclination for him not enhanced her perceptions; as it was however she knew quite well

how the land lay. But the Chevalier de Guise had guessed everything.

The Princesse de Clèves did not feel inclined to discuss this Prince and his feelings with her mother as she usually did when people were in love with her. It never occurred to her that she was being underhand in not speaking of him. But Madame de Chartres realized the whole thing only too clearly and it made her wretched. She foresaw terrible rocks ahead for the young woman, loved by such a man as M. de Nemours, if he in his turn attracted her. A few days later she had proof that a mutual attraction did indeed exist.

The Maréchal de Saint André, who was always on the lookout for a chance to show how opulent he was, implored the King to do him the honor of supping with him, bringing the two Queens, on pretext of showing them his newly finished house. He was also not at all unwilling for Madame de Clèves to see what enormous sums he had spent on it. Some days before this supper party was due to take place the King-Dauphin, who was always delicate, became ill and could see nobody, and his wife the Queen spent the whole day with him. Towards evening, feeling better, he sent for the various people who were waiting in his antechamber, and the Queen-Dauphine went back to her own rooms, where she found a few close friends, including Madame de Clèves. As it was already rather late, and she was not dressed, she decided that she would not go to the Queen that evening, but, giving orders that she was at home to nobody, she sent for her jewels. She wanted to choose

some for herself to wear at the Maréchal de Saint André's ball and others which she had promised to lend Madame de Clèves, and while they were thus occupied the Prince de Condé came in. Because of his rank no door was shut to him—he could go anywhere. The Queen-Dauphine said that, as he obviously came from the King-Dauphin, he must tell what they were all doing there.

There is a great argument going on, Madame, he replied, the Duc de Nemours against the others. He is sticking to his point so vehemently that I can see it must apply to himself; probably he has some mistress whom he cannot bear to meet in public because he says that it is always hateful to see the person you love at a ball.

What next? said the Dauphine. M. de Nemours doesn't want his lady love to go to parties? I knew that some husbands prefer their wives to stay at home, but it never occurred to me that a lover might feel like that.

Well, replied the Prince de Condé, according to M. de Nemours, there is nothing so unbearable for lovers, whether they are loved in return or not, as going to parties. He says that even if they are loved, when there is a party planned they must reconcile themselves to taking second place for several days, because the woman doesn't exist who can give her lover a thought during the business of getting a new dress—it is all-absorbing, and then this dressing up is done quite as much to impress the world in general as for the sake of the loved one. Furthermore at the ball itself it is their idea to be admired by all beholders, and the satisfaction they feel when they are

aware of looking beautiful has little or nothing to do with their lover.

Then he goes on to say that of course if love is unrequited it is a torment to see the lady at a party, since the more she is generally admired the more wretched it makes you not to be loved by her; besides which there is always the fear that her beauty will attract some other man who will have better luck with her. In short, he considers that there is only one greater agony than to see your mistress at a ball, and that is to know that she is at one where you yourself are not.

Madame de Clèves pretended that she was paying no attention to what the Prince de Condé said, but she was really listening with all her ears. She knew perfectly well that she was responsible for M. de Nemours' ideas on this subject, and especially for what he said about it being torture to a man if his mistress went to a ball without him, because it so happened that the King was sending him on a mission to the Duke of Ferrara and he would not be there for the Maréchal de Saint André's ball.

The Queen-Dauphine and the Prince de Condé were laughing together about M. de Nemours and the Queen-Dauphine said that she did not care for this point of view at all.

He did make one exception, however, ma'am, said M. de Condé, and that in favor of a ball given by the lover himself. He said that last year, when he gave one for your Majesty, his mistress did deign to attend it, although that was apparently on your account. He says that it is always a concession to a lover to go to his own party and

that a man naturally likes his mistress to see him on his own ground, entertaining the whole Court, so that he can show her how well he does it.

The Queen-Dauphine said, with a smile, M. de Nemours had every reason to be in favor of his mistress going to that ball, because in those days the title was shared by so many ladies that had they all been absent the attendance would have been rather thin.

While the Prince de Condé was telling about M. de Nemours and his views on parties Madame de Clèves conceived a great wish to stay away from the Maréchal de Saint André's ball. She told herself that it really was a mistake to be entertained by a man who loved you, and was delighted to have found such a strict reason for giving pleasure to M. de Nemours. She took the jewels which the Queen-Dauphine was lending her to wear, but, when she was showing them to her mother later on in the evening she mentioned the fact that she had no intention of using them. She explained that the Maréchal de Saint André was always letting it be seen that he was in love with her, that she had no doubt he wanted everybody to know that she would be at his party for the King and she feared that, under pretext of being a good host, he would offer her embarrassing attentions. Madame de Chartres argued for a while with her daughter, who she really thought was being too puritanical, but seeing that her mind was made up she gave in, and said in that case she must pretend to be ill in order to have an excuse for not going, because nobody would approve of her real reason and people must not be allowed to suspect it.

Madame de Clèves gladly consented to keep to her room for a few days, if by so doing she could avoid a party where M. de Nemours would not be present. He went away in ignorance of this fact, which would have pleased him so much, and only heard that she had not been there on his return, the day after the ball. Since he had no idea that his conversation at the Dauphin's could have been repeated to her it never even occurred to him that he was lucky enough to have been the cause of her staying at home.

Next day, at the Queen's, he was talking to the Queen-Dauphine when Madame de Chartres and Madame de Clèves came in and joined that princess. Madame de Clèves was dressed rather carelessly, like somebody who has been ill, but her face told a different story. The Dauphine said,

You are looking so beautiful I find it hard to believe that you have been ill. I believe that when M. de Condé told us what M. de Nemours thinks about parties he put it into your head that by going to his ball you would be conferring a favor on the Marshal, and that this must be your reason for not going.

Madame de Clèves blushed when Madame la Dauphine made this lucky guess in front of M. de Nemours, and at the same moment Madame de Chartres saw in a flash why it was that her daughter had not wanted to go to the ball. In order to conceal it from M. de Nemours she said, speaking with a great air of sincerity,

I can assure you, Madame, that your Majesty is giving my daughter credit for more than she deserves.

44

She really was ill, though indeed, had I not been there to prevent it, I feel sure she would have gone simply for the fun of seeing all those marvels at the ball last night.

The Dauphine quite believed Madame de Chartres, and M. de Nemours, rather put out, thought it sounded true enough, though Madame de Clèves' blushes made him wonder whether there had not been a good deal in what the Dauphine had said after all. As for Madame de Clèves herself, though dreadfully upset at first to think that M. de Nemours should have reason to suppose that he had been the cause of her not going to the ball, she felt a sort of vague disappointment when her mother so firmly disposed of the idea.

The conference at Cercamp had broken up but negotiations for peace still continued, and presently they took such a turn that a new conference, with the same delegates as before, was convened at Câteau Cambresis. With the absence of the Maréchal de Saint André, M. de Nemours' most dangerous rival was out of the way—dangerous rather on account of the close watch he kept over Madame de Clèves and anybody who might approach her than for any progress he himself could make in her affections.

Madame de Chartres was anxious that her daughter should not realize that she knew of her feelings for M. de Nemours, as she wanted to say various things to her without any obvious motive, and one day she began talking about him. She spoke very highly of him, saying how sensible he was never to fall in love, but to regard all relationships with women simply as pleasure, never

allowing them to develop into serious attachments.

Of course, she added, the love of his life is supposed to be the Dauphine, and he certainly does go to her rooms all the time. I think you would be well advised to avoid him as far as possible and on no account to see him alone, because in your position of intimacy with Madame la Dauphine people might say that you were acting as their go-between, and you know what a disagreeable reputation that is. In fact, if these rumors continue it might be better for you to see less of Madame la Dauphine rather than become involved in a love affair.

Madame de Clèves had never heard M. de Nemours mentioned in the same breath with the Dauphine; she was so much taken aback by what her mother told her, so positive, now, that she had been mistaken about M. de Nemours and his inclinations, that her face fell, and Madame de Chartres saw this. Just them some people arrived and Madame de Clèves went home and shut herself in her own room.

She was agitated beyond words, her mother having now opened her eyes to the fact that M. de Nemours was much more to her than it was right for him to be. She saw only too clearly that her feelings for him were exactly those which the Prince de Clèves had so often besought her to have for him; she was bitterly ashamed to think that she could have such feelings for one who was not her husband. Also she was wounded to the quick that M. de Nemours should be making use of her to further his affair with the Dauphine. This thought decided her to tell Madame de Chartres her secret.

Accordingly she went to her mother's room in the morning, but finding her unwell, with a little fever, she put off speaking to her, though, as it seemed nothing very much, she went to Madame la Dauphine after dinner as usual. The Dauphine was in her little sitting room, alone with two or three women, her greatest friends, and when she saw Madame de Clèves she said, We are talking about M. de Nemours, and saying how much he has changed for the better since he got back from Brussels. You know before he went there he had countless mistresses; really one could not approve of it because he was exactly the same to all of them—whether they were nice or not he made the best of them. Now, since his return, he simply doesn't recognize them. There has never been such a change, and it even seems to me that he is different in himself—less carefree, somehow, than he was.

Madame de Clèves did not reply. She was thinking, with shame, that had her eyes not been opened to the truth about M. de Nemours she would have taken these words as a proof of his love for herself. She felt a certain bitterness towards the Dauphine for pretending to look for reasons and to be surprised when she must have known the truth better than anybody, and could not resist letting her see a part of her thoughts so that, the other women moving away, she said to her quietly, Surely these words cannot have been meant for me? Do you think I don't realize that this change which has come over M. de Nemours is on your account?

Now that's not fair, replied the Dauphine, you know

quite well I have no secrets from you. It is true that before M. de Nemours went to Brussels he did perhaps intend me to see that I was not detested by him, but since his return it is clear that he remembers nothing that happened before, and I am bound to confess it intrigues me to know what can have made him so different. I think I shall manage, she went on. The Vidame de Chartres, his greatest friend, is in love with somebody I can influence—I shall find out the reason, I'm sure.

Madame la Dauphine's words carried conviction, and Madame de Clèves, in spite of herself, now felt more at peace with the world.

She went back to her mother and saw at once that she had become a good deal worse—there was much more fever. During the next few days her temperature was so high that she was clearly very ill indeed. Madame de Clèves, terribly worried and unhappy, never left her mother's room, and M. de Clèves also went there nearly every day, partly because he was very fond of his mother-in-law, partly to try to keep his wife from giving way to her sorrow, but chiefly for the pleasure of being with her. He was still passionately in love.

M. de Nemours, who had always liked him very much, had been especially friendly ever since his return from Brussels, and during the illness of Madame de Chartres he made opportunities for seeing Madame de Clèves, going there ostensibly in search of her husband, to take him out, and sometimes going when he knew quite well that he was not there. Then, pretending to wait for him, he would stay in the antechamber, where a

few friends were always to be found. Madame de Clèves was in and out most of the time, and her grief made her seem no less beautiful to M. de Nemours. He let her see that he felt for her sorrow, and spoke to her about it in such a way as to make her quite well aware that it was not the Dauphine he loved. She could not suppress an uneasy happiness at the sight of him, but when he was not there the thought that her love had its origins in his physical presence filled her with anguish so that she almost hated him.

Madame de Chartres now became so ill that they began to despair of her life, and the doctors told her this. She received the news with a courage worthy of her goodness and piety, sent everybody away and called Madame de Clèves to her.

My child, she said, holding out her hand, we must now part, and I grieve the more for the danger in which I see you and the need you have of me now. You are attracted by M. de Nemours—I don't ask you to confess it; I am no longer in a condition to need your confidence in order to be able to guide you. I have seen it for a long time, but hesitated to speak at first for fear of opening your eyes to a fact of which you were, perhaps, not fully aware. Now you know it yourself, only too well. You stand on the edge of a precipice and can only hold back by making a superhuman effort. You must solemnly reflect upon your duty, both to your husband and your-self, remembering that you stand to lose the reputation you have built up and which I have so much desired for you. Be brave my darling, be strong and leave this

Court. Force your husband to take you away. I know this sounds dreadfully uncivilized and difficult, but in the end it will be better than the wretchedness of a love affair.

I will give you one more reason which may help you to act as I so pray you will, and that is, if anything could trouble the happiness I hope for on leaving this world it would be the sight of you descending to the level of other women. If this misfortune is to overtake you I am glad to die and avoid seeing such a thing.

Madame de Clèves burst into tears over her mother's hand which she held tightly clasped in both of hers, and Madame de Chartres, herself much moved, said,

Farewell my child; we will say no more upon a subject which is affecting us both so deeply, but try to remember all I have told you.

She turned away when she had spoken, telling her daughter to call her women, and refused either to listen or to speak to her any more; it may be imagined in what a state Madame de Clèves left her mother's room. Madame de Chartres was now absorbed in preparations for the end, and during the two days which remained to her she refused to see the only creature in the world whom she loved, her daughter.

Madame de Clèves was terribly unhappy. Her husband never left her, and as soon as Madame de Chartres was no more he took her to the country, away from surroundings which could only intensify her grief. This grief was quite unusual in its intensity because, not only had she loved her mother deeply and felt deeply grateful

to her, but just now she felt a particular need for her help to fortify her against M. de Nemours. It seemed dreadful to be left alone at a time when she was so unsure of her own heart and when she so longed for sympathy and strength. The conduct of M. de Clèves made her more than ever anxious not to fail in her duty, and she was sweeter and more friendly to him than she had ever been. She could not bear to have him out of her sight, as it seemed to her that if she clung to him he could protect her against M. de Nemours.

The Duke visited M. de Clèves in the country and made every effort to see Madame de Clèves, but she would not receive him. She knew too well the effect he had upon her, how fatally attractive she found him, and she had resolved never to see him if she could possibly avoid it.

M. de Clèves had to go to Paris, on duty; he promised his wife that he would return the following day; nevertheless he only came back the day after that. When she saw him Madame de Clèves said,

I was expecting you all day yesterday, and now I must scold you a little bit for not coming as you promised me you would. You must have known that if I could feel any new grief in my present state it would be the death of Madame de Tournon, which I have just heard this morning. I should have felt it even if I had not known her, for it is always sad when somebody young and beautiful, as she was, dies in two days, but she happened to be one of the people who pleased me most. She always seemed to me as wise as she was good.

I was very sorry not to come back yesterday, said M. de Clèves, but I was obliged to stay and do what I could to comfort a very unhappy person. As for Madame de Tournon, if you really think that you are mourning a wise and admirable woman I advise you not to feel her death too deeply.

What is this? said Madame de Clèves. Why, I have heard you say over and over again that there was nobody at Court whom you admired more!

True enough, he replied, but women are quite incomprehensible, and the more I see of them the more thankful I am to have you. I can hardly believe my luck.

You put me too high, said Madame de Clèves, sighing. It is not yet certain that I shall prove worthy of you. But do tell me what it is that has disillusioned you over Madame de Tournon?

It is not new, he said. For a long time now I have known that she loved the Comte de Sancerre, even allowing him to hope that she would marry him.

I can hardly believe it! Do you really mean that Madame de Tournon, after all her public declarations that she could never marry again, with the views everybody knows that she has held, since her widowhood, on remarriage, has been giving hopes to Sancerre?

If he had been the only one it would not have been so extraordinary, said M. de Clèves, but at the very same time she was also making promises to Estouteville. I will now tell you the whole story.

YOU know what friends I am with Sancerre; nevertheless he was at great pains to keep it from me that two years ago he fell in love with Madame de Tournon, and neither I nor anybody else had an inkling of it. At that time Madame de Tournon seemed inconsolable for the loss of her husband and led an austere existence, withdrawn from the world. Almost the only person she ever visited was Sancerre's sister, and it was there that he fell in love with her.

One evening, when there was to be a play at the Louvre, we were all waiting until the King and Madame de Valentinois should come for it to begin, when we were told that Madame de Valentinois was unwell and that the King would not be coming. Everybody guessed that this indisposition of the Duchess was really some squabble with the King. Of course we all knew how dreadfully jealous he had been of M. de Brissac while he was at Court, but it was now several days since he had gone back to Piedmont, so we could not imagine what this was all about. I was discussing it with Sancerre when M. d'Anville appeared, and taking me on one side he told me that the King was in a pitiable state of rage and misery, that when, a few days before, he had made up his quarrel with Madame de Valentinois over M. de Brissac he had given her a ring, begging her to wear it always. Apparently, while she was dressing for

this play the King noticed that she had not got the ring, and asked her why. She seemed surprised not to see it and asked her women, who, most unluckily (or they may have been warned) said they had not seen it for four or five days. Now that was exactly when M. de Brissac left, so the King had no doubt that she had given him the ring when they said goodbye. His jealousy was revived, he flew into a rage, most unlike him, and reproached her bitterly. He then went back to his own apartments, very miserable, though whether because he thought Madame de Valentinois had sacrificed his ring or because he feared he had annoyed her I do not know.

When M. d'Anville had finished telling me this news I went directly and told Sancerre, saying at the same time that he must keep it to himself because it was a secret somebody had entrusted me with. The next morning rather early I went to my sister-in-law, where I found Madame de Tournon sitting by the bed. She had no love for Madame de Valentinois and she knew that my sister-in-law had not a good word for her either. Sancerre had been to see her after the play and had told her all about the King's quarrel with the Duchess; Madame de Tournon had come round to tell my sister-in-law, without knowing, or having forgotten, that her lover had the story from me. As soon as I appeared my sister-in-law said to Madame de Tournon that I could be trusted with what she had just told her, and, without waiting for Madame de Tournon's permission, recited word for word what I had passed on to Sancerre the evening before. Picture my amazement! I looked at Madame de Tour-

non; she did seem rather embarrassed and this made me suspicious. I had told nobody but Sancerre, he had gone off and left me at the end of the play without a word of explanation, and I remembered having heard him sing the praises of Madame de Tournon. All these things opened my eyes. I deduced without much difficulty that he was having an affair with her and that it was she whom he had visited when he left me. I felt so much annoyed to think that he had been hiding this affair from me that I said one or two things which must have shown Madame de Tournon that she had been very unwise; I went with her to her carriage and, as we parted, I said how much I envied the luck of whoever it was that had told her of the King's quarrel with Madame de Valentinois.

I then went off at once to find Sancerre and covered him with reproaches. I said I knew now that he loved Madame de Tournon, without saying how it was I had found out. He was obliged to admit it. Then I told him how I knew and he told me all about it, saying that although he was only a younger son and far from being a good match, nevertheless she had made up her mind to marry him. Nobody could be more surprised than I was. I told Sancerre that he had better marry her quickly since he could expect anything of a woman double-faced enough to have acted such a part in public. He replied that she had really been very miserable until her love for him had cured her, and that she did not want everybody to see how suddenly she had changed.

He gave me several other reasons excusing her be-

havior, which made me realize how far gone he was in love, and said that he was going to get her consent for me to be in the secret, since it was she who had given it away to me in the first place.

With some difficulty he did obtain her consent, after which I was very much in their confidence.

I have never seen a woman treat her lover better than she did; she was as frank and as delightful with him as she could be, but all the same I could not help feeling shocked at the way she kept up the pretense of being heartbroken. Sancerre was so deeply in love, and so much gratified by her behavior that he hesitated to suggest hurrying on the marriage for fear she might think that his passion was less for herself than for her money. All the same he did speak to her of it, and she seemed quite decided to marry him; she even relaxed her hermit-like existence and went out a little in the world, going to my sister-in-law at a time of day when some of the Court was likely to be found there. Sancerre hardly ever went, but those who did so every evening, and who often saw her there, thought her charming.

A little while after she had begun to go out like this Sancerre thought he noticed that her love for him was cooling. He said so to me once or twice. I did not take him very seriously, but when he told me that, far from arranging their marriage, she seemed to be putting it off, I began to think he had some grounds for his anxiety. I said it would be hardly surprising if Madame de Tournon's love, having lasted for two years, should have become rather less violent, and that he must not complain if,

without its having exactly diminished, it should now no longer be strong enough to make her marry him. This marriage, I pointed out, was going to do him no good in the eyes of the world, because it was a bad match for her and also it would injure her reputation. Under these circumstances he ought merely to wish that she should remain faithful to him without holding out any false hopes.

I also said that supposing she felt she could not marry him or even told him that she loved somebody else, he had no right to be hurt or angry but must respect her and be grateful to her.

I am only telling you to behave as I would myself, I said, because personally I value sincerity so much that though I should be miserable if my mistress, or even my wife, were to come and say frankly that she was attracted by another it would not make me bitter. I would then cast off the role of husband or lover in order to advise and sympathize with her as best I could.

At these words, which seemed to have a bearing upon her own state of mind, Madame de Clèves blushed deeply. Taken by surprise, she was very much upset, and it was some time before she recovered her self-possession.

M. de Clèves went on with his story. Sancerre, he said, spoke to Madame de Tournon as I advised him to, but she was at such trouble to reassure him, and seemed, indeed, so much offended by his suspicions, that she completely removed them. It is true that she put off their marriage until after a journey that he was obliged to

make and which was going to take rather long, but she was so nice to him until he went away, and appeared to be so miserable when the time came for his departure, that I thought, quite as much as he did, that she really loved him. It is some three months since he left, and during his absence I was so much taken up with you that I hardly saw Madame de Tournon; I only knew that he was expected back shortly. On arriving in Paris the day before yesterday I heard of her death, so I sent to his house to ask if there were any news of him and was told that he had got back the day before, the very day of Madame de Tournon's death. I immediately went to him, knowing quite well the state I should find him in, but his misery surpassed anything I could have imagined. As soon as he saw me he threw himself into my arms and burst into tears.

I shall never see her again, he said, never again. She is dead. I have never been worthy of her and soon I shall follow her.

He fell silent for a while, then wept and moaned. Never, never again, she is dead . . . and went on in this manner like somebody out of his mind. He told me that he had received very few letters from her while he was away but that this had not surprised him as he knew how much she disliked trusting anybody to take letters for her. He had never doubted that he would marry her on his return; he thought she was the most faithful person in the world and the most worthy of love and supposed himself to be tenderly loved by her. Then, just at the very moment when he thought he was to be

joined to her for ever he found that he had lost her. All these reflections plunged him into a terrible grief, and I must confess that I was deeply moved to see him in this state. At last I had to leave him in order to go to the King, but I promised to be back very soon.

On my return I was astounded to find him in quite a different mood. He was walking up and down his room as if unable to contain himself for anger—he seemed quite beside himself.

Come in, he said, look at me and see a man in total despair, a thousand times unhappier than I was just now, because I have just found out something about Madame de Tournon which to me is far worse than her death.

As I could imagine nothing worse than the death of an adored and adoring mistress I thought his sorrow must have gone to his head and I told him that I could sympathize with him while he kept it within reason but that he really must not allow himself to give way to an insane despair.

I only wish I were mad, he cried, I would welcome it as I would welcome death itself. Madame de Tournon was unfaithful to me. I find out her treachery the day after learning of her death, at a moment when my soul is prostrated with love and grief, at a moment when her memory is enshrined in my heart as perfection, perfect towards me. Now I find that I have made a mistake, that the object of my grief is unworthy—and in spite of everything I mind her death as much as if she had been faithful and her infidelity as much as if she were still alive. Supposing I had found her out before she died

I should have been so furious and so jealous that it would have stiffened me to endure her loss, but as it is my state of mind is such that I can neither forget nor hate her.

You can imagine how much these words of Sancerre's amazed me. I asked him how he knew what he had just told me and he said that a moment after I had left his room Estouteville had come to see him. This Estouteville was one of Sancerre's greatest friends, but he knew nothing about him and Madame de Tournon. He sat down and began to weep, saying that Sancerre must forgive him for having kept what he was going to tell him a secret, imploring his sympathy, since he was going to open his heart, and then saying that in seeing him Sancerre saw the person whom the death of Madame de Tournon had afflicted more than anybody in the world.

Sancerre told me, My instinct was to say that I was more afflicted than he, but the mention of this name made me quite speechless with surprise. Estouteville went on, saying that he had been in love with her for six months, that he had wished me to know it from the first but that she had so expressly forbidden him to tell me that he had not dared to disobey her. He said they had both fallen in love simultaneously but had kept it a deadly secret, he never having been seen at her house. His was the joy of consoling her for the death of her husband, he told me, and they were to have been married just at the very time of her death. She had persuaded her father to order her to marry Estouteville so that this love match should seem to be an act of filial duty on the part of one bitterly opposed to remarriage.

60

Sancerre went on: While Estouteville was speaking I could not but believe his words—it all rang too true—and the time when he said he had fallen in love with Madame de Tournon exactly coincided with the change I myself had noticed in her. But a moment later I thought he must be a liar or a visionary, and I very nearly said so. Then I thought I would clear the matter up first so I questioned him further, letting him see that I was not quite convinced; finally, when I had done all I could to assure myself of my own unhappiness, he asked me whether I knew Madame de Tournon's handwriting, and laid four of her letters and her portrait on my bed. Just then my brother came in. Estouteville, whose face was bathed in tears, was obliged to go so as not to be seen, and did so, saying that he would come back this evening to fetch these things he had left with me. As for me, I sent my brother away, pretending that I was ill, because I could not wait to look at the letters, hoping against hope to find a contradiction in them of all that Estouteville had told me. But alas! What did I not find? What tenderness, what protestations, what promises of marriage! Oh! those letters . . . ! Never in her life had she written like that to me. So you see that now I am suffering from two great sorrows at once—sorrows which have often been compared to each other but which can never have been suffered simultaneously by the same person—death and betrayal. I must confess, to my shame, that I mind her death much more than I do her faithlessness. I cannot feel that she deserved to die. If she were still here I could have the satisfaction of reproaching

her, of avenging myself by bringing home to her the injustice of her behavior . . . but I shall never see her again, he repeated, never, never again. Nothing can be worse than that; oh would that I could give her back her life! And yet, what a wish! If she came back it would be but to live for Estouteville. How happy was I yesterday, he moaned, happy! I was sadder than anybody in the world, but it was at least a reasonable sadness and I found a certain sweetness in the reflection that nothing would ever be able to console me. Today my feelings are all upside down. I am paying the same tribute of wretchedness to her sham love for me as when I thought it was real. It is impossible for me to hate or to love her memory, nor can I grieve, nor can I be consoled. One thing I beg of you, he cried, suddenly turning to me, never, never let me set eyes on Estouteville again—his very name fills me with disgust. I know quite well it was all my own fault; I should never have kept it a secret from him that I loved Madame de Tournon. Perhaps had he realized, he would not have fallen in love with her, and perhaps she would have remained faithful to me. He came to me with his sorrow and I grieve for him, ah! And with reason since he loved Madame de Tournon, was loved in return, and will never now see her again. All the same I cannot help it, I hate him, so once more I beg of you to take steps so that I may be spared the sight of him.

And upon this Sancerre returned to his tears and lamentations for Madame de Tournon, speaking to her, saying the most loving things imaginable and then pass-

ing to reproaches, hatred and imprecations against her. I saw that he was in such a desperate state that I must find somebody to help me calm him down, so I sent for his brother, whom I had just left with the King. When he arrived I had a word with him in the antechamber, explaining Sancerre's condition. We gave orders that Estouteville was not to be admitted, and then spent a great part of the night trying to make him see reason. This morning I found him more wretched than ever. His brother is with him and I came back to you.

Nobody could be more surprised by all this than I am, said Madame de Clèves, since I thought Madame de Tournon equally incapable of love and of treachery.

It would hardly be possible to have been cleverer or more false than she was, replied her husband. Just consider. At the time when it seemed to Sancerre that she was no longer the same to him he was right, because she had then begun to fall in love with Estouteville. She told Estouteville that he was consoling her for the death of her husband, and was the cause of her coming out of her retreat, while all the time Sancerre thought she was doing so on his account and because he had decided that she must stop behaving as if she were heartbroken. She made Estouteville keep their understanding a secret so that she could make it seem as if her father were forcing her to marry him, pretending that all this was due to her care for his reputation, whereas in fact she wanted to be able to drop Sancerre without giving him any cause for complaint. I shall have to go back, M. de Clèves said, to be with this poor fellow, and I think you had better

come to Paris with me. It's time you saw some people—and then there are all those visits of condolence which must be got over sooner or later.

Madame de Clèves agreed, and went back the following day. She felt much calmer about M. de Nemours; the dying words of Madame de Chartres and the grief of losing her mother had arrested the course of her feelings for him, so that she was beginning to think that she had quite got over them.

The very evening of her arrival Madame la Dauphine came to see her, and when she had assured her how deeply she shared her sorrow she said, in order to distract her from sad thoughts, that she would tell everything that had happened at the Court during her absence; she then came out with several secrets. But what I am dying to tell you, she went on, is that M. de Nemours is madly in love for certain, though he has not confided in a single soul and even his best friends cannot find out who the lady is. But this love is strong enough to make him neglect—I should really say give up—the chance of a throne.

Madame la Dauphine told all that had been happening about England. I got it from M. d'Anville, she said; it seems that the King sent yesterday evening for M. de Nemours. Lignerolle has written asking to be recalled because he says he can no longer keep up the Queen of England's interest in view of M. de Nemours' continued delay; indeed she is beginning to be offended by it since, without having actually said yes she had said enough to have induced him to risk the journey. The

King read this letter to M. de Nemours and he, instead of speaking seriously as he had done at first, did nothing but laugh and joke, mocking at Lignerolle's optimism. He said all Europe would blame him for impudence if he went to England as a suitor for the Queen's hand without being sure of success. Another thing, he added, it seems to me a very bad time to go, just as the King of Spain is making such frenzied efforts to marry this Queen. He might not be a very dangerous rival in a love affair, but surely when it comes to marriage your Majesty would hardly advise me to set myself up against him.

In this case I certainly would advise it, said the King, and it so happens that you would not find yourself against him, because I know he has other ideas; but even if he had not, Queen Mary found the yoke of Spain too disagreeable for her sister to wish it back again or to be dazzled by the prospect of uniting so many kingdoms.

Dazzled or not dazzled, replied M. de Nemours, it seems that she has ideas about being made happy by love. Some years ago she was in love with Lord Courtenay; Queen Mary loved him too, and would have married him had she not realized that the youth and beauty of her sister Elizabeth meant more to him than the hopes of the throne. Your Majesty knows that her jealousy made her clap them both into gaol, after which she exiled Lord Courtenay and made up her mind to marry the King of Spain. I feel sure that Elizabeth, now that she is on the throne, will remember this lord, and that her choice is more likely to fall upon a man whom she has already loved, who is very attractive and who has suffered

so much for her, than upon somebody whom she has never even seen.

I should entirely agree with what you say, replied the King, were Courtenay still alive, but I have just heard of his death in Padua, where he was exiled. Well, I can plainly see that we shall be obliged to arrange your wedding as we did with M. le Dauphin, and send ambassadors to marry the Queen of England.

M. d'Anville and M. le Vidame, who were present at the interview, are persuaded that it must be love which has made him change his mind about so great an enterprise. The Vidame, who is closer to him than anybody, told Madame de Martigues that he hardly knows him he is so much altered. But the oddest part of it is that he does not seem to have any special friendship, nor does he disappear at certain hours. In fact he thinks that there can be no understanding with whomever it is he loves; yet it is most unlike M. de Nemours to be in love with a woman who does not return it.

Of course these words of Madame la Dauphine were the purest poison to Madame de Clèves. How could she not but recognize this nameless lady? And how not be penetrated to the heart by learning from such a source that this Prince, to whom already she was far from indifferent, was hiding his passion for her from all the world and giving up, for her sake, the chance of a throne?

Impossible to describe her feelings. Her very soul was in a turmoil, and if Madame la Dauphine had been watching her carefully she would have seen at once that the subject of this conversation was not indifferent to her,

but, as she had no inkling of the truth she prattled on thoughtlessly enough: M. d'Anville, who, as I said, told me all this, thinks I know more than he does—he puts my attractions so high that he is sure I must be the only person alive who could bring about such a change in M. de Nemours.

These last words threw Madame de Clèves into a new sort of agitation.

I am inclined to agree with M. d'Anville, she said. It seems to ring true. Surely, it would require nothing less than a princess, Madame, like yourself, to make the Queen of England seem to be of no account.

Madame la Dauphine replied, If I knew that I would tell you, and furthermore if it were so I should know it. A love of that sort cannot be hidden from the person who is responsible; indeed she would be the first to notice it. M. de Nemours was never especially attentive to me, but even so there is a gulf between his present and his former manner. I can assure you that it is not I who have made him indifferent to the throne of England. When I am with you, she added, I forget everything. I am supposed to go and see Madame now. You know that the peace is practically concluded, but perhaps you do not know that the King of Spain has refused to pass any of its clauses except on condition that Madame should marry him instead of his son Don Carlos. Our King could hardly bring himself to it, but in the end he accepted, and just now he has gone to announce the news to Madame. I think she will be inconsolable; after all it is not a very agreeable prospect—marriage with a

man of the King of Spain's age and temperament, especially for one so gay, young and beautiful, with hopes of marrying a young prince who, though she had never seen him, had great attraction for her.

I am not sure the King will find her as accommodating as he hopes; he told me to go and see her, because he knows that she is fond of me and he thinks I might be able to influence her. After that I have a very different visit to pay, since I go to rejoice with Madame the King's sister. All is now arranged for her marriage with the Duke of Savoy; he will be here shortly, and nobody of that Princess's age can ever have been so delighted to marry. This Court is going to be more crowded and more resplendent than we have ever known it, and in spite of your mourning we count on you to show the foreigners that our beauties are by no means to be despised.

On these words the Dauphine left Madame de Clèves, and the next day the whole world knew of Madame's marriage. The day after that the King went with the Queens to call on Madame de Clèves. M. de Nemours, who had been awaiting her return with the greatest impatience and who longed to speak with her alone, waited to pay his visit until an hour when it was unlikely that more people would arrive and when, on the contrary, people would be leaving her rooms. His plan succeeded, and just as the last guests were going he arrived. Madame de Clèves lay on her bed; it was very hot weather. The sight of M. de Nemours gave her a color which did not make her less beautiful to look at. He sat facing her in that sort of timidity which betokens a genuine passion,

and remained for a while unable to utter a word. Madame de Clèves was no less overwhelmed, so that they kept a long silence. At last M. de Nemours spoke, condoling with her in her sorrow. Madame de Clèves, who would have been glad to keep the conversation to that topic, spoke at length of the loss she had sustained, saying that though time might take the edge off her grief such a deep impression had been made on her character that her whole outlook would henceforth be altered.

He replied, Great sorrow can effect great changes in the soul and so can violent passion, and as for me, I don't know myself since I got back from Flanders. Many people have seen this change, and Madame la Dauphine spoke of it again yesterday.

Yes, said Madame de Clèves, I do seem to have heard her mention it.

I am not sorry that she sees it, said M. de Nemours, though I could wish that she were not the only one to do so. There are certain people to whom a man can only express the love he feels by quite indirect methods, but though he may not be brave enough to show it he does at least hope that it may be apparent to his beloved how little he wishes to be loved by anyone else, that no beauty, whatever her rank, can touch his heart, and that even a throne would not tempt him if he could only have it at the price of never seeing her again. Women generally gauge the extent of a man's love by the trouble he takes to seek their company and to please them, but none of that is any trouble if they are the least bit amiable. It is far more difficult to resist the pleasure of being with them

69

and to avoid their company lest the world in general and they themselves should guess the truth. The sign of a real attachment is the change it produces—for instance, if it should make somebody indifferent to ambition and to pleasure who all his life has been given over to these two things.

Madame de Clèves understood perfectly that these words were meant for her. She felt that she ought to make some reply, that she ought to stop him, and yet at the same time she ought not to know what he meant. In short it seemed to her that it was her duty both to speak and to remain silent. She found M. de Nemours' remarks both pleasing and offensive; they confirmed what Madame la Dauphine had put into her head. She found in them a certain chivalry and respect but also too much boldness and frankness. The Prince attracted her so much that she was no longer mistress of her emotions, and the most veiled remarks from a man who exercises such an attraction are more agitating than an open declaration from another. So she did not reply, and M. de Nemours would have noticed her silence, and might have drawn a not unfavorable conclusion from it, had not the arrival of M. de Clèves put an end both to the conversation and to his visit.

THE Prince had come to give his wife news of Sancerre, but she was not really very much interested in the latest instalment of that story, and was so entirely absorbed by what had just occurred that she was hardly able to conceal her absence of mind. As soon as she had a chance to think it over quietly she realized how mistaken she had been in supposing that she now felt nothing but indifference towards M. de Nemours. His words had made as deep an impression as he could have hoped, forcing her to believe in his love, and since his actions were suited to his words she was left in no doubt whatever.

Now that she could no longer deceive herself with hopes that she was not in love with him her only preoccupation was never to give any sign by which he could guess that she was. This would be difficult indeed—how difficult she knew too well already—and she knew that her only chance of success lay in avoiding the Prince.

Owing to her mourning it was quite natural for her to lead a more retired existence than usual, so she made it an excuse never to go where he might see her. She was in very low spirits, but her mother's death seemed to be the reason and nobody looked for another.

M. de Nemours was in despair at hardly ever seeing her, and when he realized that she was not to be found at assemblies, or at any of the amusements where the whole

Court gathered, he could not bring himself to go to them either. He pretended to have a passion for hunting, and arranged hunting parties on those days when the Queens held their receptions. Then for a long time he was unwell, and this gave him an excuse to remain at home and avoid going out to places where he knew he would not find Madame de Clèves.

M. de Clèves fell ill at about the same time, and Madame de Clèves never left his room, but when he was better and beginning to receive visitors, M. de Nemours, under pretext of still feeling weak himself, spent a large part of every day with him, so that Madame de Clèves felt that she could no longer stay there, although the first few times that he came she had not the strength to leave, it was too long since she had seen him.

The Prince gave her to understand, by saying things which seemed meant for everybody, but which she recognized as being on the same lines as what he had told her in her room, that he went hunting to indulge in his dreams, and avoided receptions because she was never there. At last she carried out her resolution of leaving her husband's room whenever he came to it, but only by dint of doing great violence to her feelings; the Prince saw that she fled from him and was deeply affected.

At first M. de Clèves paid no attention to his wife's behavior, but presently he noticed that she refused to stay in his room when he had visitors and he spoke to her about it. She replied that in her opinion it was not seemly for her to spend every evening with the younger members of the Court and begged him to agree that she should

lead a more retired life than when her good mother had been there, making it possible, by her presence, for her to do all sorts of things which, at her age, it would be hardly proper for her to do alone. M. de Clèves, who was by nature extremely indulgent to his wife, was not so on this occasion, and he told her that there could be no question of such a change in her habits. She was on the point of telling him that all the world was saying M. de Nemours was in love with her, but she did not feel able to pronounce his name, and besides she was ashamed to use a false argument and to conceal the truth from a man who valued her so highly.

A few days later, the King being with the Queen at her hour for receiving, the talk was all of horoscopes and the prophecies, and opinions were greatly divided as to how much they could be believed. The Queen believed in them; she maintained that it was impossible not to see a great deal of truth in a science which had accurately predicted so many things, while others said that out of an endless number of prophecies very few came true and that it was clearly a question of luck.

I used to be very curious about the future, said the King, but I have been told so many lies and improbabilities that now I feel sure one cannot know the truth. Some years ago a man came here with a great reputation as an astrologer. Everybody went to him, I among others, without saying who I was. I took M. de Guise and Descars with me, making them go in first, but it was to me that the astrologer addressed himself, as if he knew that I was their master. Possibly he recognized

73

me, but then he said a thing which could not have applied to me if he had. He told me I should be killed in a duel. Then he told M. de Guise that he would be killed from behind, and Descars that his head would be bashed in by the kick of a horse. M. de Guise was rather angry as the prophecy seemed to accuse him of running away, nor was Descars exactly pleased to think that he would come to such an unfortunate end. In short we all left very much dissatisfied with this astrologer. I don't know what may be in store for M. de Guise and Descars, but it seems hardly likely that I shall be killed in a duel. The King of Spain and I have just made peace, but even had we not I doubt whether we would have fought a duel or that I would ever have called him out as my father the King called out Charles V.

Those who had been upholding astrology ceased to do so on hearing of the misfortune which had been foretold for the King, agreeing that it was perfectly incredible.

M. de Nemours said, Nobody could believe less than I do. Then he turned to Madame de Clèves who was beside him and said in a low voice, I have been told that the person in all the world for whom I feel the most violent, respectful passion is one day to make me happy by her sweetness to me. So you may well imagine how much I believe in prophecies.

Madame la Dauphine, thinking that, because M. de Nemours' first words were spoken out loud, he was telling some false prophecy that had been made to him, asked what he had said to Madame de Clèves. A man

with less presence of mind might have been taken off his guard by this remark, but without a moment's hesitation he replied,

I was just saying that once I was told of a tremendous destiny which awaited me, so great that I would not even dare aspire to it.

If you were really told that, Madame la Dauphine said with a smile, thinking of the English affair, you ought not to despise astrology but rather find reasons for supporting it.

Madame de Clèves knew exactly what the Dauphine meant, and she also knew that the great destiny of which M. de Nemours spoke had nothing to do with being King of England.

Now, quite a long time having elapsed since the death of her mother, she was obliged to begin going out again and take up her duties at the Court. She saw M. de Nemours at Madame la Dauphine's, he often came, with friends of the same age in order to pass unnoticed, to her husband's, and she saw him then, but never could she see him without an agitation of which he was perfectly well aware. However much she sought to avoid his eye, to speak less with him than with others, she gave herself away by something in her first movement, and the Prince felt certain that she was not indifferent to him. A man with less penetration might not have noticed anything, but he had already been loved so many times that he could hardly fail to recognize the symptoms. He knew that the Chevalier de Guise was his rival, and the Chevalier knew that M. de Nemours was his. He was the only

man at Court to have unmasked this fact, his own interest in the matter having made him see more clearly than other people. So the knowledge of each other's feelings introduced a bitterness between them which appeared in everything. Without ever exploding into a quarrel, they always took opposite sides, were it at tilting, at jousting, or at any of the King's other amusements; in fact their rivalry was so great that it could not be concealed.

The English business was much in Madame de Clèves' thoughts; it seemed to her that M. de Nemours would never be able to hold out against the advice of the King and the representations of Lignerolle. She saw, with some distress, that the latter had not yet returned, and she awaited him impatiently. If she could have known his exact movements they would have indicated how matters stood, but the very reason for her curiosity was also a reason for concealment, so she merely informed herself about the beauty, talents and character of Queen Elizabeth. Somebody had brought one of her portraits to the King, and Madame de Clèves thought it had more beauty than she had hoped; she could not help remarking that it must flatter the Queen.

I don't think so, said Madame la Dauphine, who was there. They say this Princess is a beauty and that she has a more independent mind than most people; she has been held up to me as an example ever since I can remember. If she is like her mother, Anne Boleyn, she must be charming, for few women have been as attractive in every way as she was. I have often heard what a lively and

original look she had, and that she had nothing in common with other English beauties.

Was she not born in France? said Madame de Clèves. I seem to have heard so.

The people who believe that are wrong, replied Madame la Dauphine, and I will tell you her story in a few words. She came of a good English family; Henry VIII was in love with her sister and her mother; in fact some people think that she was his daughter. She came over here with the sister of Henry VIII who married King Louis XII. When her husband died this Princess, who was young and romantic, was very sad at having to leave the French Court, and Anne Boleyn, who was of the same mind as her mistress, could not decide to go. The late King was in love with her, and she stayed on as lady in waiting to Queen Claude. Then the Queen died, and the King's sister Madame Marguerite, Duchesse d'Alençon, afterwards Queen of Navarre, whose stories you have read, took her into her household, when, under the influence of that princess, she became tainted with the new religion. Presently she went back to England, where she charmed everybody with those French manners which other nations find so agreeable; she sang well and danced beautifully. She became Lady in Waiting to Catherine of Aragon; then King Henry VIII fell madly in love with her.

Now Cardinal Wolsey, the King's favorite and prime minister, who had had hopes of the papacy, was dissatisfied with the Emperor for not supporting him in his ambition, so he decided in revenge to make a matri-

monial alliance between his King and the King of France. He put it into Henry's head that his marriage with the Emperor's aunt was null and void and proposed to him that he should marry the Duchesse d'Alençon, whose husband had just died. Anne Boleyn, who was ambitious, saw in this divorce the way to a throne. She began by filling the King of England with impressions of Luther's religion, then persuaded our late King to take up the cause of his divorce with Rome, in the hopes of marrying him to the Duchesse d'Alençon. Cardinal Wolsey got himself sent to France, ostensibly on other business but really with a view to negotiating this affair, but his master would not hear of it and sent orders to Calais forbidding him to speak of the marriage. On his return from France Cardinal Wolsey was received with royal honors; no favorite can ever have carried pride and vanity to such lengths. He brought off a meeting of the two Kings and this took place at Boulogne. They entertained each other in turns with extraordinary magnificence, exchanging replicas of the suits they had had made for themselves. I remember hearing that the suit our late King sent Henry VIII was of crimson satin trimmed with triangles of pearls and diamonds, and a robe of white velvet embroidered with gold.

After a few days at Boulogne they went on to Calais. Anne Boleyn was lodged with King Henry VIII; she had a queen's retinue and François I gave her presents and honors exactly as if she had been one.

Finally, after having been in love for nine years, Henry married her without waiting for the dissolution of his

first marriage, which he had long been demanding from Rome. The Pope immediately pronounced fulminations against him and Henry was so much irritated by this that he declared himself head of the Church and dragged the whole of England into that unfortunate change of religion in which you see her now. Anne Boleyn did not enjoy her glory for long. The death of Catherine of Aragon having, as she thought, assured her position, she was with the whole Court one day watching her brother, Lord Rochfort, tilting at the ring, when the King was suddenly overcome with such an access of jealousy that he left for London in the middle of the match. Once there he ordered that the Queen, Rochfort, and several others whom he suspected of being her confidants or lovers, should be arrested. Although his jealousy seemed to have been born at that very moment it had really been inspired some time since by Lady Rochfort, who could not bear the great intimacy between her husband and the Queen and pretended to the King that it was a guilty passion. The result was that he, already being in love with Jane Seymour, soon had but one idea in his head, how best to get rid of Anne Boleyn. In less than three months he had caused the Queen and her brother to be tried and executed and had married Jane Seymour. After her he had several more wives, whom he either killed or repudiated, among others Catherine Howard, the confidante of Lady Rochfort. They had their heads cut off together, so in the end she was punished for the crimes she had wished onto Anne Boleyn. Henry VIII finally died himself after becoming quite enormous.

All the ladies who were present while Madame la Dauphine told of these events thanked her for teaching them so much about the English Court, and among them was Madame de Clèves, who could not help asking her a few questions about Queen Elizabeth.

The Queen-Dauphine was having miniatures painted of all the Court beauties, to send to her mother the Queen. The day that Madame de Clèves' portrait was finished Madame la Dauphine came to spend the evening with her after dinner. M. de Nemours did not fail to be there; though he never let it be seen that he sought the company of Madame de Clèves, he never let a chance go by of being with her. That day she was looking so beautiful that he fell in love all over again, yet he dared not gaze while her hair was being combed out for fear that people might notice the joy it gave him to look at her. Madame la Dauphine asked M. de Clèves for a miniature he had of his wife, to compare it with that which was just finished, and everybody expressed their opinions on one and the other. Madame de Clèves told the artist to make a little adjustment to the coiffure of the one they had just brought in, and, in order to do so, the artist took it out of its box, worked on it for a while, and then put it back on the table.

Now M. de Nemours had long wished to possess a portrait of Madame de Clèves, and when he saw the one belonging to M. de Clèves he could not resist the temptation of stealing it from a husband whom he thought tenderly loved. It seemed to him that among so many people crowded together suspicion would not

fall on him more than on another. The Dauphine was sitting on the bed speaking in a low voice with Madame de Clèves, who stood by her. Madame de Clèves could see M. de Nemours through a curtain which was only half drawn; he had his back to the table at the foot of her bed and she saw how, without turning his head, he deftly picked something off the table. She guessed at once that this must be her portrait and she was very much upset. The Dauphine noticed that she was no longer listening to her and asked out loud what she was looking at. At her words M. de Nemours turned round and met the eyes of Madame de Clèves still upon him, and he thought very likely she had seen what he had just done. Madame de Clèves was not a little embarrassed. It would have been reasonable to ask to have her portrait back again, but if she did so out loud it would proclaim to everybody there his feelings for her, while to do so when alone with him would have looked like an invitation for him to speak of his love. Finally she judged it best to leave him the portrait, happy to accord him a favor since she could do so without him knowing it. M. de Nemours, noticing her embarrassment and more or less aware of its cause, went up to her and whispered, If you saw what I dared to do, be kind . . . ignore it. It is all I ask of you. Having said this he left, without waiting for her to reply.

The Dauphine left to go walking, followed by her ladies. M. de Nemours shut himself in his room, for the happiness of owning a portrait of Madame de Clèves was too great to be borne in public. He was enjoying all

the most agreeable feelings that love can bring; he loved the most charming woman of the whole Court and was making her love him back whether she would or not; he noticed in everything she did the agitation and shyness which love induces in very young people.

That evening they sought the miniature high and low. As the case was still there in its proper place nobody suspected that it might have been stolen but they thought it must have slipped down by accident. M. de Clèves was very sad at his loss and when it had once more been looked for in vain he said to his wife, jokingly, that she must have some secret lover to whom she had given it, or who had stolen it, since none but a lover could want the picture without its case. These words, though he said them laughingly, made a deep impression on Madame de Clèves and filled her with remorse. She reflected upon the violence of the inclination which was pushing her towards M. de Nemours. She knew that she could hardly control herself, she knew also that Lignerolle was back, that she no longer feared the English business, that she no longer suspected Madame la Dauphine, in short that her defences were breaking down and there could be no safety for her except in flight. But since it was not in her power to fly she felt at the end of her tether and ready to fall into what seemed to her the worst wretchedness, that of letting M. de Nemours see what her feelings were for him. She thought of all Madame de Chartres had said when dying and how she had advised her to do any-thing, resort to any device, however difficult, rather than embark on a love affair. Then she remembered what M.

de Clèves had said, when speaking of Madame de Tournon, about sincerity, and she thought it was perhaps her duty to confess to him. She considered this for a long time, then was amazed that she could ever have had such a mad idea, after which she fell back into a state of complete indecision.

Peace was now signed. Madame Elizabeth, in spite of the repugnance she felt, made up her mind to obey the King her father; the Duke of Alba was nominated to come, as proxy for the Catholic King, and marry her. The Duke of Savoy was coming to marry the King's sister—the two weddings were to take place very soon, together—and the King's great preoccupation was to mark them with a series of entertainments at which his Court should appear to its best advantage. Suggestions were made for everything that was most wonderful in the way of plays and ballets, but the King wanted something more spectacular.

So he decided upon a tournament, open to foreigners, at which the people of Paris would be the audience. The Princes and young nobles took up the idea with delight, especially the Duke of Ferrara, M. de Guise and M. de Nemours, who all surpassed at this form of sport. The King chose these three to stand with him against all challengers.

It was now proclaimed throughout the kingdom that, on the 15th of June in the City of Paris, his most Christian Majesty, together with the Princes Alphonso d'Este, Duke of Ferrara, François de Lorraine, Duc de Guise and Jacques de Savoie, Duc de Nemours, would hold an

83

open tournament against all comers. The first combat to be on horseback in the lists, with double armor to break four lances and one for the ladies, the second with swords, one against one or two against two, as the judges should direct, and the third on foot, three thrusts of the pike and six of the sword. The champions to provide swords, lances and pikes as chosen by the combatants. Whoever failed to manage his horse to be put out of the lists. Four judges of the field would give orders, and decide the value of the prize, which would be carried off by whoever performed best and broke most lances. All the combatants, whether French or foreign, to be obliged to touch one, or more if they wished, of the shields which were to hang on a pillar at the bottom of the lists, where a herald at arms should be ready to enroll them, according to their rank. The combatants to send a gentleman with their shields to be hung up three days before the tournament, or they would not be admitted without leave of the champions.

A great lists was set up near the Bastille, stretching from the Château des Tournelles, crossing the rue Saint-Antoine, and ending at the royal stables. There were two sides of scaffolding and amphitheatres with covered boxes, forming as it were galleries, very pretty to look at and capable of holding an infinite number of spectators. The Princes and nobles thought of nothing but their accoutrement and how to appear as splendid as possible, also how best they could introduce something charming, and appropriate to the lady of their choice, into mottos and cyphers.

A few days before the Duke of Alba's arrival, the King played a game of tennis with M. de Nemours, the Chevalier de Guise and the Vidame de Chartres. The two Queens were there to watch them with all their ladies, including Madame de Clèves. As they were leaving the tennis court, at the end of the game, Châtelart went to the Queen-Dauphine and told her that he had got a love letter which had fallen out of M. de Nemours' pocket. The Dauphine, who was always interested in everything that concerned M. de Nemours, told Châtelart to give it to her. She took it and followed the Queen her mother-in-law who had gone with the King to see the work which was being done at the lists. Presently the King sent for some horses which had just come, and in spite of the fact that they were not properly broken in he insisted upon mounting them, giving one to each of his companions. The King and M. de Nemours found themselves on the two wildest, who began trying to hurl themselves at each other. M. de Nemours, fearful of hurting the King, pulled his horse sharply back against a pillar of the riding school, hitting it with such violence that the shock unseated him. They ran to him, thinking he must be badly hurt, and Madame de Clèves thought him more hurt than anybody else did, owing to the special interest she took in him. She did not think of concealing her agitation, and the expression on her face, would have given her away to a man much less in love than the Chevalier de Guise. As it was, he saw only too clearly, being far more interested in the condition of Madame de Clèves than in that of M. de Nemours.

This Prince was completely stunned by the blow, and remained for some time with his head lying limp against those who held him. When at last he lifted it his eyes fell first on Madame de Clèves. He saw, written upon her face, the concern she felt for him and he gave her a look which showed her that he was deeply touched. Then he thanked the Queens for their marks of kindness towards him, excusing himself for having appeared before them in such a condition. The King told him to go away and rest.

Now that Madame de Clèves had got over her fright she began to reflect on the signs of it that had escaped her, nor did the Chevalier de Guise leave her for long in the hopes that nothing had been noticed. Giving her his hand to lead her away from the lists he said, I am more deserving of pity than M. de Nemours so you must forgive me if I appear to forget the deep respect I have always had for you and say how sad I am at what I have just seen. This is the first time I have ever been bold enough to speak to you, as it will be the last. I must leave this place, seek death, perpetual exile, anything rather than stay here now that I can no longer even console myself by thinking that all those who lift their eyes to you are as hopeless as I.

Madame de Clèves could only reply to this with a few incoherent words as though she had not quite grasped the Chevalier's meaning. At any other time she would have been angry with him for speaking of his feelings for her, but now she merely felt miserable to think that he had noticed what hers were for M. de

Nemours. The Chevalier de Guise was so certain of them, and so penetrated with sadness, that from then on he decided never even to think of being loved by Madame de Clèves. He came back to an idea he had long had in mind—the conquest of Rhodes—which seemed glorious enough to turn his thoughts from the other conquest. When death removed him from this world, in the flower of his age and already famous in his generation, he said that he only had one regret, which was not having been able to carry out this plan, which he had prepared so carefully that he supposed it to have been infallible.

Madame de Clèves went to the Queen on leaving the lists, much preoccupied by what had just occurred. Presently M. de Nemours came in, splendidly dressed and evidently quite unaffected by his accident, so happy indeed at what he thought he had noticed that he was even gayer and more attractive than usual. Everybody was surprised when he appeared, and all hastened to ask how he felt, except Madame de Clèves, who stood by the chimney piece pretending not to have seen him. The King came in, and seeing him with the others called him over to tell about his accident. M. de Nemours passed by Madame de Clèves and murmured to her, I noticed today that you were concerned about me, but it is not that which I most deserve.

Madame de Clèves had been afraid that the Prince must have noticed the weakness she had for him, and his words showed her that she was not mistaken. It was a terrible blow to her to feel that she was now no longer able to hide her feelings and that she had allowed the

Chevalier de Guise to become aware of them. She was also displeased that M. de Nemours should know everything, though this displeasure was not unmixed with a sort of sweetness.

The Queen-Dauphine, most impatient to find out what was in the letter which Châtelart had given her, said to Madame de Clèves, Do go and read this letter addressed to M. de Nemours; it looks as if it must be from the new mistress for whose sake he has left all the others. If you can't read it now, keep it and bring it back to me while I am going to bed. Having said this Madame la Dauphine left Madame de Clèves, who was so utterly taken aback that for a moment she stood transfixed. Then in wild impatience she went to her own rooms, though it was long before her usual time for retiring. She held the letter in a hand that trembled, her thoughts were confused, nothing seemed clear to her, and she found herself in an agony such as she had never experienced or dreamed of. As soon as she was back in her sitting room she opened the letter and read as follows:

I have loved you too dearly; I cannot let you go on thinking that the change which you see in me is due to any fickleness of mine and I wish you to know that it is the result of your own unfaithfulness. You may well be surprised that I should speak of this unfaithfulness which you have so cleverly hidden from me, since I also have kept from you the fact that I knew all about it. I am surprised myself that I was able to prevent you from noticing that I knew. Nobody has

88

ever suffered as I do. I thought you were violently in love with me, as I was with you. I made no secret of it. I allowed you to see its full extent, only to find that you are deceiving me and that you love another; everything goes to show that you are sacrificing me to a new mistress. I knew it the day of the tilting; I feigned illness to hide my despair, and became ill indeed, for my body was unable to endure the shock. When I began to feel better I went on pretending to be ill in order to have an excuse for neither seeing nor writing to you. I wanted time in order to make up my mind how I ought to behave with you; twenty times I made the same resolutions and twenty times unmade them again, but in the end, thinking you unworthy to witness my misery I decided to hide it from you. I wanted to wound your vanity by letting you see my love die a natural death, thinking that this would cheapen the sacrifice you were making of it. I had no wish for you to wear my love as an ornament to make you more desirable. I resolved that my letters should be lukewarm and flat, to show her to whom you passed them on that you were no longer loved. I could not bear her to enjoy the delightful knowledge that she had won a victory over me, nor to sweeten her victory with my reproaches and despair. Then I thought that merely to break with you would not punish you enough, that it would be but a slight wound for me to stop loving you once you loved me no more. No. You must be forced to love me again if you were to feel the misery, as I was feeling it so bitterly, of being

loved no more. If anything could rekindle the feelings you once had for me, I thought, it would be the knowledge that mine for you were dead, especially if I could make you realize it while pretending to keep it from you as though I was afraid to confess it.

This is what I finally decided—but what a painful decision and how difficult, once I had seen you again, to put into practice! A hundred times I could have burst out with tears and reproaches; only the fact that I was still unwell enabled me to hide my misery from you. After a while the pleasure of deceiving you as you were deceiving me helped me to keep it up; nevertheless I did myself so much violence in telling and writing my love to you that you noticed a change in me before I meant you to. You were hurt by it, you complained. When I tried to reassure you my manner was so unnatural that you felt more certain than ever that I had stopped loving you; in short I had done exactly what I meant to do. Contrary as ever, you had but to realize that I was putting a distance between us to begin a pursuit. Now I tasted all the joys of vengeance; it seemed to me that you loved me better than you ever had while I let you see that I loved you no more. I had reason to suppose that she for whom you had left me was in her turn abandoned; I also had reasons for thinking that you had never mentioned me to her. Nevertheless neither your return nor your discretion can make up for your fickleness.

Once your heart has been divided between me and

another, once I have been deceived, there is no pleasure left in being loved by you as I felt I deserved to be. So I have made this resolution, which seems to you so surprising, never to see you again.

MADAME DE CLEVES read and re-read this letter many times without even being conscious of having read it at all, conscious indeed of one thing only, that M. de Nemours' love for her was not what she had supposed, that he loved others, and deceived them even as he was deceiving her. This was indeed a sad discovery for one of her temperament, madly in love as she was, and who had allowed not only the object of her love, now shown to have been unworthy, to guess at it, but also somebody else whom she had treated badly on his account. She felt a stinging distress, exacerbated by the events of that day; it even seemed to her that she could have borne M. de Nemours' love for another had she not given him reason to believe that he was possessed of hers. But in this, of course, she was quite mistaken, since the unbearable pain that she was suffering was nothing more nor less than jealousy, accompanied by all its attendant horrors. She understood from this letter that M. de Nemours had a longstanding love affair. The writer of it seemed clever, distinguished, worthy of love, and more controlled, she thought, than she herself could ever be. She envied the courage which had enabled this lady to hide her true feelings from M. de Nemours. By the last words of the letter she saw that the writer thought that she was loved; then it occurred to her that the discretion which the Prince had shown with her, and which

she had found so touching, might simply have been due to his passion for this other lady and a fear of displeasing her. So she went on, torturing herself with every fancy which could increase her despair, with self reproaches and with memories of her mother's advice. Why had she not been quite firm with M. de Clèves and insisted upon retiring from society, or even followed her impulse of confessing that she was attracted by M. de Nemours? She thought now that it would have been far better to have confessed to a husband of whose goodness she was well aware and who had every reason to have kept the secret, than to have had it discovered by a deceiver who for all she knew was only making use of her, only wanted her love out of vanity. The torture she was suffering, even if it drove her to extremities, was nothing to the knowledge that M. de Nemours loved another while she had disclosed her love for him.

She quite forgot that Madame la Dauphine had told her to go there at bedtime; she pretended to feel ill, and went to bed. When M. de Clèves came in from being with the King he was told that she had gone to sleep, but she was really very far indeed from that peaceful state of mind which leads to sleepiness. She read and reread the letter, working herself into a misery, and so passed the night.

Madame de Clèves was not the only person whose rest had been disturbed by that letter. It was the Vidame de Chartres who had lost it, not M. de Nemours, and he was extremely worried. He had spent the evening with M. de Guise, who gave a big supper party for his brother-

in-law the Duke of Ferrara and all the young people of the Court. It so happened that during supper there was talk of letter writing, and the Vidame said that he had on him the most beautifully written letter in the world. They all begged him to show it, but he refused, upon which M. de Nemours said that of course it was non-existent and he had only mentioned it from vanity. The Vidame answered that this was trying his discretion very high but that all the same he would not show the letter; he would however read out certain bits of it which would be enough to show that it was such as few men had ever received, and as he spoke he made to bring out the letter, but could not find it. He searched in vain and the others began to taunt him, but he was so evidently upset that they stopped talking of it. He was the first to leave the party, and hurried to his room to see whether he had not left the missing letter there. While he was still hunting for it high and low the Queen's first footman came to him, sent by the Vicomtesse d'Usez, who thought he should be warned of what everybody was saying in the Queen's apartments. It seemed that a love letter had fallen out of his pocket while he was in the tennis court, that most of its contents were already being bandied about, that the Queen was most curious and wanted to read it, and that one of her gentlemen whom she told to get it for her had replied that he had last seen it in the hands of Châtelart. The first footman told the Vidame de Chartres various other things which made him so uneasy that he went there and then to a great friend of Châtelart and got him out of bed, though it

was an extraordinary hour to go asking for letters. He did not even say who wanted the letter or who had lost it. Châtelart, having made up his mind that it was M. de Nemours' letter and that this Prince was in love with Madame la Dauphine, was in no doubts as to who it was that kept asking for it. He answered, with spiteful relish, that he had given the letter to the Queen-Dauphine. His friend went back to the Vidame with this reply, which worried him more than ever. For some time he could not make up his mind what to do; finally he thought that the only person who could help him out of his difficulty was M. de Nemours. He went off to find him and came into his room just as day was breaking. The Prince was in a peaceful sleep, what he had seen of Madame de Clèves the day before having given him none but pleasant thoughts. He was astonished at being woken up by the Vidame, and asked why he had come like that to spoil his sleep. Was it in revenge for the things he had said at supper? But then he saw, from the Vidame's face, that something very serious indeed had brought him there.

I have come to confide in you the most important affair of my life, he said. But you won't be particularly grateful to me; the fact is I need your help, and I know quite well that if I had told you these things without it being absolutely necessary to do so I should have forfeited your esteem. That letter of which I spoke yesterday—it had fallen out of my pocket, and it is of the greatest importance that nobody should know it was addressed to me. It fell in the tennis court yesterday, and

many of the people who were there have seen it. Now you were there too and I beg and implore of you to say it was you who lost it.

M. de Nemours said, with a smile, It's quite obvious that you think there is nobody with whom I should have a misunderstanding if I allowed it to be supposed that I receive letters of this sort, or you could never make such a proposition.

Please, please listen to me without joking, said the Vidame. If you have a mistress, which I don't doubt, though I have no idea whom she may be, you can easily explain everything to her—I will give you all the proofs. Even if you do not explain, the worst that can happen is that you will have a short misunderstanding, whereas I, by this accident, will compromise a woman who has loved me deeply—a really good woman—and besides that I shall draw upon myself an implacable hatred which will cost me my fortune and probably more besides.

I don't understand everything you are saying, said M. de Nemours, but you have opened a peephole and I am beginning to guess that rumors I have heard about a certain great Princess and her interest in yourself are not without foundation.

They are not, and would to God they were, replied the Vidame, because then I should not find myself in this situation. I had better tell you everything so that you may see how much I have to fear. Ever since I first came to Court the Queen has always been particularly good to me and I have had reason to think that she had a special feeling for me, though there was nothing I could actually

lay my finger on and I have never thought of her otherwise than with deep respect. As a matter of fact I was in love with Madame de Thémines, a lady whom you only have to see to realize that love for her, if she returned it, and in my case she did, could be something very deep. Nearly two years ago now, when the Court was at Fontainebleau, it happened several times that I was talking with the Queen at a time of day when there were very few people about. I could see that she found me good company and she entered into everything I said. One day, among other things, we spoke of trusting people, and I said that I completely trusted nobody, having found it always led to regrets, and that I knew a great many things which I kept to myself. The Queen remarked that this raised me in her estimation, since she knew nobody in France who could keep a secret, and it was a thing she found particularly thwarting because she could no longer indulge in confidences. She added that it is a necessity for everybody, and especially for people, like her, in high places, to have a person to whom they can speak freely. The next few days she often came back to this topic, and even told me some rather private things which were happening. I felt that she wanted to know my secrets and to tell me hers, and this made me fond of her since I was touched that she should single me out in this way; I became much more attentive to her than I had ever been before. One evening the King and all the ladies went riding in the forest, but she, not feeling very well, stayed behind and I with her. She went down to the lake, leaving her equerries so that she could walk with

more freedom. She walked up and down for a while and then, coming to where I was she told me to follow her, saying, I wish to speak with you, and you will see by what I tell you that I am your friend.

Having spoken thus she stood still, and looking earnestly at me she continued, You are in love, and since you confide in nobody you imagine, perhaps, that your love is not known. Known it is, however, and by those whom it closely concerns. You are watched, the place where you meet the lady has been noted and a plan is afoot to surprise you there. I do not know who she is, I only want to protect you from misfortune.

Now just think what a trap the Queen was setting for me, and how difficult it was not to be caught in it. She wanted to know if I really was in love, she asked no questions, she did not appear to be speaking either from curiosity or with some end in view but simply as if it was for my own good. All the same I soon got to the bottom of the affair. I was in love, with Madame de Thémines, but although she loved me in return I was not in the happy position of having some special place where I met her and where I might be afraid of discovery, so I knew quite well that the Queen could not be speaking of her. I also knew quite well that I was carrying on another affair with another woman, who was less beautiful than Madame de Thémines and less virtuous, and it was not impossible that my meeting place with her had been found out, but as I did not care for her much it was quite easy to protect myself from that danger by not seeing her any more.

So I decided that I would confess nothing to the Queen but on the contrary would assure her that I had long ago given up the sort of woman of whom I could have hopes, since they all seemed to me more or less unworthy of an honest man's love, and that nowadays it would take something on a very different plane to compromise me.

You are not telling the truth, said the Queen. The opposite of what you say is really the case and I know it. After the way I have spoken you owe it to me not to conceal anything. I want us to be friends, but in that case you must not hide your affairs from me. That is the price, and you can have two days to think it over, but afterwards be careful what you say to me and remember that if later on I find you have been untruthful I will never forgive you as long as I live.

On these words the Queen left me without waiting for me to answer. You may imagine that I was full of what she had said, and the two days she had given me to make up my mind did not seem any too long for such a decision. I saw that she wanted to find out whether I was in love, and that she was hoping to hear I was not. I foresaw certain consequences of the decision I was to take and was not a little flattered at the idea of a special relationship with the Queen, a Queen, at that, whose physical charms were still considerable. On the other hand I was in love with Madame de Thémines, and although I was being unfaithful to her in a way with this other woman I mentioned, I really could not decide to break with her altogether. I was clearly exposing myself

to danger by deceiving the Queen, and it would be very difficult to take her in successfully—all this I saw, but still could not bring myself to refuse what fortune was offering me. I decided to risk the consequences of my bad behavior; I broke with the woman whose affair with me might have been found out and I hoped that my love for Madame de Thémines could be kept a secret.

At the end of the two days which the Queen had given me I came into her room and, in front of all the ladies who were there, she said, with a serious look that quite surprised me, Have you seen about that business I wanted you to do for me? What is the truth?

Yes, Madame, I replied, and it is just as I told your Majesty.

Then come this evening—I will write down the time —and when I see you I will give you your instructions.

I bowed low, without answering, and did not fail to go at the hour she gave me. I found her in the gallery with her secretary and a few ladies in waiting. When she saw me she took me to the far end of the gallery, saying, So you have nothing to tell me after all these deliberations? I should have thought you might have been frank with me considering my attitude towards you.

Exactly so, Madam, I replied, and that is why I have nothing to say, and I can swear to your Majesty, with my respectful duty, that I am not in love with any lady of this Court.

I believe you because I wish to do so, said the Queen, and I wish it because I need your undivided allegiance; your friendship would be useless to me if you were in

love. Lovers are never trustworthy; you cannot depend upon their discretion. They are too distracted to be whole-hearted about anything and their mistress necessarily comes first. None of this fits in with what I want of you. So remember that if I give you all my confidence it is only because I have your word that you are free. I want you to be entirely at my disposal. You must have no friend, either male or female, of whom I do not approve; your only preoccupation must be how to please me. You will lose nothing thereby; I shall watch over your affairs better than you ever could, thinking myself well rewarded for anything I can do if the hopes I place in you are ful-filled. I have singled you out to hear the tale of all my vexations and to help me smooth them over. You have probably guessed that I am not happy, though I may seem to put up with the King's infatuation for Madame de Valentinois without minding very much. The fact is that I find it intolerable. She rules the King, she is unfaithful to him, she despises me, and all my servants are on her side. My daughter-in-law the Queen, proud of her own beauty and of her uncles' prestige, owes me no allegiance. The Connétable de Montmorency is the real overlord of this King and his kingdom. He hates me and has given evidence of his hatred that I can never forget. The Maréchal de Saint André is as forward as a young favorite can be, yet behaves better to me than the others do. You would be sorry for me if you knew all the details of my misfortune. Up to now I have dared to confide in nobody, but I have faith in you. Please never let me regret it; please be my one consolation.

As she finished speaking the Queen's eyes were quite red, and I was so deeply touched by her confidence that I was ready to throw myself at her feet. Since then I have known all her secrets. She does nothing without consulting me, and the relationship between us exists to this very day. Now, however preoccupied I may have been by my understanding with the Queen, I was not able to overcome my instinctive inclination for Madame de Thémines and I clung to her very much. I thought that she had begun to love me less, but this fact, instead of curing my love for her, as I should have allowed it to do had I been wise, positively redoubled it, and I behaved so rashly that the Queen got wind of my attachment. People of her race are very prone to jealousy—perhaps, indeed, this Princess had stronger feelings for me than she quite realized herself. Be this as it may, the rumor that I was in love made her so sad and so uneasy that I thought I was completely finished as far as she was concerned. In the end however I managed to reassure her by dancing attendance and uttering many false vows, though I could never have taken her in for long had I not been estranged from Madame de Thémines, in spite of myself, by the great alteration in her. She let me see that she no longer loved me; I felt so sure that this was the truth that I stopped teasing her and left her in peace.

Some time afterwards she wrote me this letter which I have lost. Then I saw that she had found out the affair I had been having with that other woman I mentioned to you, and that this was the reason for her change of heart.

My affections being no longer divided, the Queen now

became quite pleased with me, but, since the feelings I had for her were not such as to make me incapable of any other attachment, and since love cannot be harnessed by will power, I fell in love again, this time with Madame de Martigues, whom I used to find very attractive in the days when she was Ville-Montais and a lady of the Queen-Dauphine. I have reason to suppose that she does not absolutely hate me, and she is pleased by my great discretion in the matter, though she does not know why it is so necessary. The Queen is now assailed by new suspicions, not indeed of Madame de Martigues but very annoying ones all the same. Madame de Martigues is always with the Queen-Dauphine so I go there now much more than I used to and the Queen has got it into her head that I am in love with that Princess. The fact that the Queen-Dauphine is equal in rank with her, while she is infinitely younger and more beautiful, has plunged her into a furious jealousy and hatred of her daughter-in-law which she can no longer conceal.

The Cardinal de Lorraine has now begun to meddle in the affair. He has wanted for some time to take my place with the Queen and I have no doubt that, under pretext of bringing her and the Dauphine together again, he has nosed out the truth, and is doing me all sorts of harm without the Queen realizing what he is up to.

So this is the present state of affairs. Just imagine what will happen if it becomes known that this letter belonged to me. Apart from what the Queen will think of my trustworthiness when she sees that I was lying to her about Madame de Thémines and at exactly the same time

lying to Madame de Thémines about somebody else, there is Madame de Martigues to be considered. I am very much in love with Madame de Martigues and Madame la Dauphine is certain to show her the letter, which she will suppose to have been written quite lately. So I shall be in trouble with everybody, including the woman I love and the woman I fear. You do see why I beg and implore you to say that it was your letter, and to get it away from Madame la Dauphine.

Yes, I see plainly, replied M. de Nemours. It would hardly be possible to be in a worse muddle and I am bound to say you deserve it. I have been accused in my time of unfaithfulness and of conducting several affairs at once, but I should never have even dared to consider taking on what you have. How could you have hoped to keep both Madame de Thémines and the Queen? Or have expected to be able to deceive the Queen—an Italian as well as a Queen, that is to say full of suspicions, jealousy and pride. Then, when by good luck rather than good management you find yourself free from entanglements, what do you do? You take on new ones. How could you possibly have expected to be able to love Madame de Martigues, at this Court, without the Queen noticing anything? Your one idea ought to have been to wipe out the shame she must have felt at taking the first step. Of course she is violently in love with you—this is not a thing for you to say or for me to ask, but it is perfectly obvious. Now she is suspicious, and all the facts are against you.

I don't think it's for you to read me this sermon, the

Vidame interrupted him. Considering your own experiences you really might be a little more easy going. I quite admit that I am in the wrong, but now do think of some way out of this horrible situation. All I can think of is that you must go and see the Queen-Dauphine as soon as she is awake and ask for the letter as though you had lost it.

I have already told you that I find this a most peculiar proposition, said M. de Nemours, and one which in my special circumstances is full of difficulties. Furthermore, if the letter was seen falling out of your pocket, it won't be very easy to pretend that it fell out of mine.

I thought I had mentioned that the Queen-Dauphine was told that it fell out of yours, said the Vidame.

M. de Nemours, foreseeing at once in this case a misunderstanding with Madame de Clèves, said furiously, Do you mean that Madame la Dauphine has been told that I dropped the letter?

Yes, that's it, said the Vidame. When your servants and mine went for our clothes in one of the rooms at the tennis court it happened that several gentlemen of the two Queens were there. The letter fell and the gentlemen picked it up and read it aloud. Some thought it was yours and some thought mine, and Châtelart, who took it and whom I have been asking for it, said that he gave it to the Queen-Dauphine as yours. On the other hand, unfortunately, those who spoke of it to the Queen said that it was mine, so it would be quite easy for you to do as I ask and get me out of this muddle.

M. de Nemours had always been very fond of the

Vidame de Chartres, the more so on account of his relationship with Madame de Clèves, but all the same he felt that he could not risk her hearing of this letter in connection with himself. He was deeply considering the whole question when the Vidame, who guessed, more or less, what was on his mind, said, I see what it is: you are afraid of a misunderstanding with your lady love; indeed I could almost suspect that she is none other than Madame la Dauphine, except that M. d'Anville never seems at all jealous of you. But in any case I can't allow my peace of mind to be bought at the expense of yours and I will give you means of proving to the lady that this letter was meant for me and not for you. There. That is a note from Madame d'Amboise, Madame de Thémines' friend, who knows all about her feelings for me and who, in this note, asks me to return the letter I have lost. My name is on it, and the contents prove beyond a shadow of doubt that the letter she is asking for is the one that has been found. I give you this note; you can show it to your mistress and put yourself in the right with her. But please do not lose a single moment; promise me that you will go this very morning and see Madame la Dauphine.

M. de Nemours gave his word and took the note. But before going to see Madame la Dauphine he had something much more urgent to do. He had no doubt but that Madame de Clèves would already have heard about the letter and it was unbearable to him that somebody he loved so deeply should have reason to suppose that he was involved with another woman. So as soon as he

thought she might be awake he sent a message saying that only an affair of great urgency could cause him to ask for the honor of an interview at such an extraordinary hour.

Madame de Clèves was still in bed, bitterly upset by the thoughts which had been tormenting her all night, and great was her surprise when she heard that M. de Nemours was asking for her. She felt so resentful that she did not hesitate to send word that she was unwell and could not speak with him. The Prince did not find this refusal very upsetting; a little coldness, when it is caused by jealousy, is never a bad sign. He went to M. de Clèves' room, told him that he had called on his wife and that he was particularly sorry that she could not receive him since he had something important to tell her which concerned the Vidame de Chartres. In a few words he gave the gist of the matter to M. de Clèves who then immediately took him into his wife's room. Had she not been in the dark, Madame de Clèves would hardly have been able to conceal her agitation or her great surprise that M. de Nemours should come into the room like this, escorted by her husband. M. de Clèves told her that it was all about a letter, that her help was wanted in the interests of the Vidame, that he himself had to be off at once as the King had just sent for him, but that he would leave her and M. de Nemours to consider what had best be done.

So M. de Nemours found himself alone with Madame de Clèves just as he had hoped.

I come to ask you whether Madame la Dauphine has

spoken to you of a letter which Châtelart put into her hands yesterday?

I believe she did say something about it, replied Madame de Clèves, but I don't see what this letter can have to do with my uncle. I assure you he is not even mentioned in it.

It is quite true that he is not mentioned, said M. de Nemours. Nevertheless the letter was written to him and it is of the greatest importance for him that you should get it back from Madame la Dauphine.

Madame de Clèves answered, I don't quite understand. Why should he mind this letter being seen? And why should his name be used for getting it back?

If you would be good enough to give me a few minutes, Madame, I will explain everything and also tell you of certain matters which are so important to the Vidame that I would never even have told M. le Prince de Clèves had I not needed his help to come and see you.

I don't think it's very much good telling me anything, said Madame de Clèves, rather sharply. It would be more to the point to go and see the Queen-Dauphine and tell her the great interest you take in this letter, because she was given to suppose that it belongs to you.

M. de Nemours had never in his life been so gratified by anything as he was now by the bitterness of Madame de Clèves, so much so that he did not feel in any particular hurry to justify himself.

I have no idea what Madame la Dauphine has been given to suppose, he said, but the letter has absolutely nothing to do with me; it was written to the Vidame.

Very well, replied Madame de Clèves, I believe you, but the Queen-Dauphine happens to have been told a different story, and she may find it hard to see why M. le Vidame's letters should come falling out of your pockets. So unless you have some good reason, of which I know nothing, for lying to the Queen-Dauphine, I think, if I were you, I should own up.

There is nothing to own up to, he said. It's not my letter, and if I wanted to persuade somebody of this fact that person would not be the Queen-Dauphine. Let that be, however. The point is that M. le Vidame is involved in all this and there are one or two things which I think you ought to know, if you will allow me to tell you of them.

Madame de Clèves said nothing so he assumed that she was willing to listen and went on to tell her as shortly as possible what he had learnt from the Vidame. She listened to the whole story, which was after all very sensational, with a coldness that gave the impression either that she had not believed a single word or that she found it perfectly uninteresting. Her attitude did not change until M. de Nemours mentioned Madame d'Amboise's note, addressed to the Vidame de Chartres, which was to prove that all he had been telling her was true. Madame de Clèves knew that this woman was the friend of Madame de Thémines, and at last she found a semblance of truth in what M. de Nemours was saying which made her think that, after all, it was perhaps not his letter. Suddenly and in spite of herself her icy indifference began to melt. M. de Nemours, having read out the contents

of the note, handed it to her saying that perhaps she would recognize the writing. She could not help taking it, looking at the superscription to see that it was addressed to the Vidame, and then reading it through to make sure that the letter which was asked for was indeed the one in her own possession. M. de Nemours told her everything he could think of to persuade her, and as it is not difficult to believe what we wish to believe, he ended by convincing Madame de Clèves that the letter had never had anything to do with him.

Now she began to discuss the whole matter with him —the difficult and even dangerous position of the Vidame, the naughtiness of his behavior and how best he could be helped. She marvelled at the Queen's conduct; she confessed to M. de Nemours that she had the letter all the time—in short, now that she believed him innocent, she was ready to enter, in an open and happy frame of mind, into an affair to which at first she had hardly listened. They decided that they must not return the letter to Madame la Dauphine for fear that she might show it to Madame de Martigues, who knew Madame de Thémines' handwriting and whose interest in M. le Vidame would be sure to make her guess that it was addressed to him. They also thought that it would be best not to tell the Queen-Dauphine the part about her mother-in-law the Queen. Madame de Clèves, pretending that this was all for her uncle's sake, was more than ready to keep any secrets told her by M. de Nemours.

This Prince did not spend the whole time talking about the Vidame and his affairs; indeed the freedom with

which they were speaking might have made him bolder than he had ever dared to be hitherto had they not been interrupted by a message from the Dauphine commanding Madame de Clèves' immediate presence. So M. de Nemours had to leave her. He went to find the Vidame to tell him that it had seemed more sensible, on leaving him, to go to Madame de Clèves who was his niece than to go straight to the Queen-Dauphine. He was not at a loss for excellent reasons why the Vidame should approve of this proceeding, and for hoping that all would end well.

Madame de Clèves dressed as quickly as she could to go to the Queen-Dauphine. Hardly had she entered her room than this Princess beckoned her up and said in a low voice, I have been waiting these two hours for you, and never, never have I been so much at a loss how to conceal the truth than I have this morning. The Queen has heard people talking about that letter I gave you yesterday and she imagines that the Vidame de Chartres was the one who dropped it. You know that she takes a good deal of interest in him. So she has been asking for the letter and sent to Châtelart for it; he replied that he had given it to me, then they came to me, explaining that it was a charming example of letter writing and the Queen wanted to see it. I did not dare say that you had it; I was afraid she would think I had given it to you because of the Vidame being your uncle and that there was some understanding between him and me—I have already noticed that she can hardly bear it when he sees me often. So I said that the letter was in a dress that I was wearing

yesterday and that whoever has the key of my wardrobe had gone out. Quick now, give me this letter, so that I can send it to her, but first I must read it to see if I know the writing.

Madame de Clèves was even more embarrassed than she had expected to be. I don't know what you can do, Madame, she said, because M. de Clèves, to whom I gave it to read, has given it back to M. de Nemours. He came round this morning imploring him to get it from you, and M. de Clèves was unwise enough to own that he had it and then weak enough to give in to the prayers of M. de Nemours.

You have put me in the most embarrassing situation possible, replied Madame la Dauphine; it was really very wrong of you to give that letter to M. de Nemours without asking my permission, since I was the one who gave it to you. Now what do you suggest for me to say to the Queen, and what is she going to make of all of this? She will think, quite naturally, that the letter was to do with me and that there is something between me and the Vidame, and nothing will ever persuade her that this letter really belonged to M. de Nemours.

I am in despair at having caused you this trouble, said Madame de Clèves, but really M. de Clèves is to blame and not me.

Not at all, said the Dauphine. It's your fault for giving him the letter. No other woman in the world runs to her husband with all the things she knows.

Yes, I was in the wrong, said Madame de Clèves, but

let us see how the fault can be put right instead of examining whose it was.

At this the Queen-Dauphine asked her if she remembered more or less what there was in the letter and she replied that she knew it well, having read it more than once.

In that case, said the Dauphine, you must go and get it written out in an unknown handwriting and I will send it to the Queen. She won't give it to people who have seen it already, but should she do so I will swear it's the one Châtelart gave me and he won't dare contradict me.

Madame de Clèves agreed to this the more willingly since she thought she would send to M. de Nemours for the real letter so that it could be copied word for word, with a similar handwriting, and then, she thought, the Queen would be quite taken in. As soon as she was back in her own room she told her husband of Madame la Dauphine's predicament and begged him to send for M. de Nemours, which he did, and Nemours came with all haste. Madame de Clèves told him what she had already told her husband and asked for the letter, but M. de Nemours replied that he had already given it back to the Vidame de Chartres, who had been so delighted to have it and to find himself out of danger that he had sent it then and there to Madame de Thémine's friend. Madame de Clèves was now in a new difficulty, but at last, after a great deal of consultation, they decided to write the letter from memory; they shut themselves up to work at it, giving orders that nobody was to be admitted and sending all M. de Nemours' people away. The at-

mosphere of mystery and secrecy thus created had no little charm for the Prince, and even for Madame de Clèves herself. Her conscience was reassured by the presence of her husband and also the feeling that all this was in the interests of the Vidame de Chartres, and she was able to enjoy the pleasure of seeing M. de Nemours without a qualm; she had never been like this before, in such a state of unclouded happiness, and the joy she was feeling made her more lively and playful than M. de Nemours had ever seen her so that his love for her was increased a hundredfold. Since he also had never enjoyed himself so much his spirits soared and every time Madame de Clèves began thinking about the letter and how to write it, the Prince, instead of seriously helping her, did nothing but interrupt and make jokes. As Madame de Clèves entered into his mood they had been there a long time and the Queen-Dauphine had sent already twice to hurry up Madame de Clèves, before half the letter was written.

M. de Nemours forgot all about his friend's interests and was delighted to spin out the time while he was enjoying himself so much; Madame de Clèves was not exactly bored herself and she also quite forgot the interests of her uncle. By four o'clock the letter was hardly finished, and so badly written, the handwriting so hopelessly different from that which they were supposed to be copying, that the Queen could hardly have failed to guess the truth, and, in fact, she was not the least taken in. In spite of all the trouble that was taken to convince her that the letter was meant for M. de Nemours she remained

quite certain in her own mind, not only that it belonged to the Vidame de Chartres but also that the Queen-Dauphine had something to do with it, and that these two had an understanding. This idea greatly increased her hatred for the Princess. She never forgave her and persecuted her until the moment when she obliged her to leave France. As for the Vidame de Chartres, he was finished as far as the Queen was concerned. It may be that the Cardinal de Lorraine already had an ascendancy over her, or possibly the affair of the letter, which showed her that she had been deceived, put her in the way of unravelling various other deceptions which the Vidame had already practiced on her; in any case he was never able to make it up with her, their liaison came to an end and she finally encompassed his ruin at the time of the Amboise conspiracy in which he had become involved.

When the letter had gone to Madame la Dauphine, M. de Clèves and M. de Nemours went off together, leaving Madame de Clèves alone. As soon as she no longer felt herself carried away by that special joy of being with the person one loves, she came to her senses, as it were out of a dream, and began to reflect, with some surprise, on the extraordinary difference between her present state of mind and that of the previous evening. She saw herself as she had been, cold and acid towards M. de Nemours all the time she supposed that Madame de Thémines' letter had been meant for him, and then, as soon as he had managed to convince her that the letter had nothing to do with him, what a happy calm had replaced her bitterness! When she thought how,

only the day before, she felt as if she had committed a crime because she had let him see a solicitude for him which was really no more than ordinary compassion, and that now by her bitterness she had made it quite clear that she was jealous in a way that only lovers are jealous, she hardly recognized herself.

Then she went on to think that M. de Nemours was perfectly well aware that she knew of his love, and he must have noticed how this not only made no difference to her behavior with him, even in the very presence of her husband, but that, on the contrary, she had never been so favorably inclined towards him before and that it was she who had made M. de Clèves send for him so that they could spend an afternoon alone together. She began to feel as if she had an understanding with M. de Nemours, as if she was being unfaithful to a husband who least in the world deserved such behavior, and she was bitterly ashamed. She felt ashamed, too, at appearing so unworthy in the eyes of her lover. But what seemed to her most unbearable of all was the memory of her state of mind during the night and the agony she had been in when she thought that M. de Nemours was being unfaithful to her and that he loved another.

Up to this time she had been quite ignorant of the deadly anxiety which can be caused by suspicion and jealousy; her only care had been how to prevent herself from falling in love with M. de Nemours and she had not yet begun to fear that he might love another. Now, although the suspicions aroused by the letter had been wiped out, they had given her an idea of what jealousy

really is—an emotion she had never so far known. Why, she wondered, had it never occurred to her how unlikely it was that such a man as M. de Nemours, whose dealings with women had always been lighthearted in the extreme, should be capable of a sincere and lasting attachment? She felt that it was nearly impossible for her to be content with any love that he could give her.

But even if I could be, she said to herself, what do I want with it? Do I want to allow it? Do I want to respond? Do I want to enter into a love affair? Do I want to fail M. de Clèves? Do I want to fail myself? And finally do I want to expose myself to the cruel remorse, the deadly sadness which love brings in its train? I am conquered and overcome by an attraction which is luring me on in spite of myself. Vain are my resolutions; I thought yesterday all that I am thinking today but today my actions are the exact contrary of yesterday's resolutions. I must tear myself away from M. de Nemours' presence. I must go to the country. However strange my journey may seem I must go and if M. de Clèves insists upon preventing me, or on knowing my reasons, perhaps I shall be obliged to hurt him and to hurt myself by telling him.

So she made up her mind, and stayed at home the rest of the evening without going to find out from Madame la Dauphine what had become of the forged letter. When M. de Clèves came in she told him that she wished to go to the country, that she was not well and felt the need for fresh air. M. de Clèves, who could see by her radiant looks that there was not much the matter with

her, made fun of this journey and said that she must be forgetting the marriages of the Princesses and the great tournament. She had not too much time as it was, he said, to see about her clothes if she was to compete with the other women. None of this made her change her mind, and she begged her husband to allow her to go to Coulommiers while he was at Compiègne with the King. Coulommiers was a beautiful house which they were building with much loving care, about a day's journey from Paris. M. de Clèves consented to this, and she went, planning to stay there longer. The King left for Compiègne, where he was only going to be a few days.

M. DE NEMOURS had felt it deeply that he had not seen Madame de Clèves since the delightful afternoon which he had spent with her and which had greatly raised his hopes. His longing to see her was so great that it gave him no rest, so much so that when the King came back to Paris he decided to go to his sister the Duchesse de Mercoeur who lived in the country not very far from Coulommiers. He suggested to the Vidame that he might go there with him, thinking that they could then visit Madame de Clèves together, and the Vidame accepted willingly.

Madame de Mercoeur was overjoyed to receive them and her only thought was how they could best be amused. She offered them all the pleasures of the countryside. While they were out stag hunting, M. de Nemours got lost in the forest and when he was asking his way back he discovered that he was quite near Coulommiers. As soon as he heard the word Coulommiers he went off at full gallop in the direction which was shown him, without really knowing what he intended to do when he got there. Presently he found himself, in the forest, going down well kept rides at random, thinking that they probably led to the house. At the end of these rides he came upon a pavilion consisting of one big room flanked by two closets, of which one opened on a flower garden with only a fence between it and the forest, while the

other looked down a great avenue into the park. He went into this pavilion and would have stayed there admiring its beauty had he not seen M. and Madame de Clèves, accompanied by a crowd of servants, coming up the avenue. As he had not expected to see M. de Clèves, whom he had left with the King, his first instinct was to hide, and he went into the closet which gave on to the flower garden, thinking he could get out by a gate he saw open to the forest. But when he realized that Madame de Clèves and her husband were settling down in front of the pavilion while their servants stayed in the park, unable to get to where he was without going through the place where M. and Madame de Clèves were sitting, he could not resist staying to look at the Princess. The temptation of hearing what she had to say to a husband who made him more jealous than any other rival was too much for him.

He heard M. de Clèves say to his wife, But why don't you want to come back to Paris? What is there to keep you in the country? For some time now you have had a taste for solitude which I find very odd and which makes me unhappy since it separates us. You seem to me rather low, more so than usual, and I am afraid something is worrying you.

No, I have nothing on my mind, she replied, looking rather embarrassed, but there is always so much going on at the Court, and one is always in such a crowd that it cannot but be tiring both for body and soul. I must sometimes have a little rest.

Rest, he replied, is not intended for people of your age.

The Court is your home; you have no cause to be over-tired, and I am afraid that you must like being separated from me.

If you think that, you are being very unfair to me, she replied, with increasing embarrassment. But I do beg of you to leave me here. If you could live here alone with me, and without the mob which always surrounds you, that would make me very happy.

This look and these words show me only too plainly, cried M. de Clèves, that you have a reason for wishing to be alone. I don't know what it can be and I beg you to tell me.

He went on like this for some time, pressing her to give a reason, but without success, though she defended herself in a way which still further aroused his curiosity, by sitting silent, her eyes on the ground. At last she suddenly looked at him, saying,

Do not force me to admit something for which I have not the strength, although several times I have planned to do so. Just reflect however upon one thing. Is it prudent for a woman of my age, mistress of her own behavior, to remain unprotected in the midst of that Court?

I think you hardly know what you are hinting at, cried M. de Clèves, something I would not even name, for fear of shocking you.

Madame de Clèves did not answer, and her silence confirmed his suspicions. You say nothing, he said, which is as good as to admit that I am right.

Alas! she cried, throwing herself to the ground at his knees. I will make a confession such as no husband

has ever heard, which the innocence, both of my conduct and of my intentions gives me strength to make. It is quite true—I have reasons for leaving the Court. I want to escape the dangers into which people of my age sometimes fall. I have never given any sign of weakness and if you allow me to retire from the Court I have no fear that I shall give any, just as I would have had no fear if Madame de Chartres had still been here to help me. However dangerous the decision, I take it gladly so as to keep myself worthy of you. If my thoughts are disagreeable to you I beg you a hundred pardons, and at least I can promise never to displease you by my actions. Consider whether what I am about to do does not indicate a greater love and esteem for a husband than anybody ever had before. Guide me, pity me and love me still, if you can.

While she spoke, M. de Clèves sat with his head in his hands, quite beside himself and without lifting his wife from her knees, but when she had finished and he saw her there, her face wet with tears, so admirably beautiful, he felt that he could die of grief. He lifted her up and kissed her.

Oh Madame, he said, you must pity me too; I deserve it, and please forgive me if in the first moments of the terrible grief I am feeling I have not responded as I should have to such behavior as yours. You seem to me more worthy of esteem and admiration than any woman, but at the same time I am the saddest man who has ever lived. I loved you from the first moment I set eyes on you; your severity could not quench my love, nor the pos-

her confession !!

session of you, and it is as strong today as ever. But I have never been able to make you love me, and now I see you are afraid of loving somebody else. Who is he, this lucky man who makes you afraid? Since when has he attracted you? What is the way he has found to your heart? The thought that nobody could touch it was my consolation for not having done so myself. Now that another has succeeded where I have failed I am jealous as a husband and as a lover, but the husband's jealousy can no longer exist after such an action as yours. It is too noble not to reassure me; even as your lover I feel consoled by it. The faith you have in me is priceless; you think highly enough of me to believe that I will never abuse your confidence and you are right—I will never abuse it and I will love you none the less. You have made my unhappiness by the greatest proof of fidelity that a woman can give her husband; now, finish the story, tell me who it is you wish to avoid?

I beg of you not to ask me that, she said. I have decided never to tell you; it would not be wise for me to do so.

Have no fear, said M. de Clèves. I know too much of the world to imagine that friendship for a husband has ever prevented anybody from falling in love with a wife. One must hate the person but one cannot complain; so once more, Madame, I conjure you to tell me what I want to know.

You can't make me do that, she replied. I am strong enough to keep silent when I think it right. My confession was not made from weakness; it required more

courage than would have been needed to keep it to my-self.

M. de Nemours did not miss a word of this conversa-tion, and what Madame de Clèves said made him hardly less jealous than her husband. He was so madly in love with her that he supposed that everybody else was too, imagining many more rivals than in fact there were, and now he cast about to find whom Madame de Clèves could possibly mean. He had had the impression that she found him quite attractive, but this was based on such trivialities that it did not even occur to him that this passion, so desperate as to require so desperate a remedy, could have been awakened by him. He was so much carried away that he hardly knew what was happening, and he could not forgive M. de Clèves for not insisting more upon his wife naming the man.

M. de Clèves did make every effort to find out, and after he had tried in vain to make her tell it she said,

I think you ought to be contented with my frankness without asking anything more. Please do not make me sorry for what I have done, but rest assured that I have never, by any action, disclosed my feelings and nothing has ever been said to me which could offend me.

M. de Clèves suddenly burst out, I can't believe you. I remember how embarrassed you seemed the day your portrait was lost. You gave it away, Madame. You gave my portrait I loved so much and to which I had every right—mine! You have not been able to hide your feel-ings. You are in love; it is known. Only your virtue has so far been your guarantee.

How can you possibly think that there is anything false in a confession such as I have freely made, she cried. You must believe me, I have paid dearly for the confidence I ask of you. Please believe that I never gave my portrait. It is true that I saw somebody take it, but I did not want it known that I saw for fear of having things said to me which up to then the person had not dared to say.

Then how do you know this person loves you? asked M. de Clèves. What signs of love has he given you?

Spare me, she said, from having to tell you certain little things which I am ashamed to have noticed and which made me only too well aware of my own weakness.

You are right, he said, it isn't fair of me. You must always refuse when I ask you things like that, but you must not be angry because I ask.

Just then some of the servants who had been waiting round about in the rides came and told M. de Clèves that a gentleman had just come with a message from the King ordering him to be in Paris that evening. M. de Clèves was obliged to go and could say no more to his wife. He implored her to come the next day and begged her to believe that, although he was very sad, he still loved and admired her as much as ever.

As soon as the Prince had gone, and Madame de Clèves was alone, she began to consider what she had done and she was so appalled by it that she could hardly believe it was true. She thought that by her own action she had thrown away her husband's heart and esteem and

had dug herself a pit from which she would never be able to escape. She asked herself how she could have done such a dangerous thing, but she did not know, and she hardly thought that she had meant to. The fact that such a confession was unheard of made her realize all its dangers. But when she thought that although the remedy was desperate it was really the only way of defending herself against M. de Nemours, it seemed that she had not taken too great a risk and that she need not be so remorseful. She spent the night full of indecision, worry and sadness, but at last some peace came to her and she even found a certain sweetness in having given proofs of fidelity to a husband who so deeply deserved it, and who had shown his love and confidence by the way in which he had received her confession.

Meanwhile M. de Nemours left the spot where he had overheard a conversation so closely connected with himself and plunged back into the forest. Madame de Clèves' words about the portrait put new life into him, showing that this man she did not hate was he himself, and for a while he gave himself up to this joy, but the mood did not last long, because he soon realized that the very incident by which he had discovered that it was he who had touched her heart must also prove to him that he could not hope to receive any sign from her, and that he would never have his way with a woman who could do such an extraordinary thing. All the same it pleased him to think that he had reduced her to this extremity and he felt that there was something glorious in having won the love of a woman so different from the rest of her sex.

So his happiness, which was great, and his unhappiness were about equal. He was overtaken by nightfall while yet in the forest and had some trouble in finding his way back to the château of Madame de Mercoeur, only arriving there as day was breaking. It was rather difficult to explain what had delayed him; he got out of this as well as he could and went back to Paris with the Vidame that very day.

M. de Nemours, obsessed with his passion and the surprise of what he had overheard, now fell into a not unusual indiscretion—that of talking in general terms of a particular experience. During the journey he brought the conversation round to the subject of love, emphasizing the pleasure of loving a person who was really worthy of it. He spoke of the curious manifestations it sometimes produces and finally, unable to bottle up his amazement at what Madame de Clèves had done, he told the Vidame the whole thing, without mentioning any names or saying that it had anything to do with him. However the Vidame guessed this at once, from the way in which he spoke and the warm admiration he expressed, and he urged him to own up, saying that he had realized for some time that M. de Nemours was violently in love and that it was hardly fair of him to distrust a man who had entrusted him with all the secrets of his own life. But M. de Nemours was too much in love to be able to confess it, and had always kept it from the Vidame in spite of the fact that he was the greatest friend he had at Court. He replied that one of his friends had told him this story under a vow of secrecy; he begged

the Vidame never to repeat it and this the Vidame promised. All the same M. de Nemours now repented of having said so much.

M. de Clèves went back to the King, and he was stricken to his very heart with a mortal sadness. Few husbands can ever have loved their wives so passionately, or felt such admiration for them. He did not admire her any the less for what he had just learnt, but in a different way, and he was deeply preoccupied trying to guess who it was who had been able to win her heart. He thought first of M. de Nemours, as the most attractive man at the Court, then of the Chevalier de Guise and the Maréchal de Saint André, both of whom he knew had paid attentions to her and had hoped to please her; he felt sure that it must be one of these three and did not seek any further. When he arrived at the Louvre, the King took him to his study and said that he had chosen him to accompany Madame to Spain as he could think of nobody who would perform this mission so well and nobody who would bring so much credit to France as Madame de Clèves. M. de Clèves received the honor of this choice as he should, and indeed he saw it as something which would take his wife from the Court without any apparent change in her mode of life; nevertheless the departure was still too far off to provide a way out of his difficulty. He wrote at once to Madame de Clèves, telling her what the King had just said, and repeating that he insisted upon her coming back to Paris. She duly came, and when they saw each other they were both overcome by an extraordinary sadness.

M. de Clèves spoke like the honorable man he was, and worthy of what she had done. I have no misgiving over your conduct, he said. Your character and your virtue are stronger than you think, so it is not any fear of the future that makes me so unhappy, but my failure to arouse a feeling in you where another has succeeded.

She replied, What can I say? I die of shame when I speak with you. Please try and spare me these cruel conversations; tell me what I must do. Arrange matters so that I see nobody—this is all I ask of you—but do not make me talk any more about something which puts me in such a shameful light, unworthy of you and of myself.

You are quite right, he answered. I am taking advantage of your sweetness and your trust in me. All the same you must feel sorry for the state of mind into which you have thrown me, and remember that whatever you may have said, what you have not said is a certain name, and I am dying of curiosity to know it. I am not going to ask, but I cannot help telling you that I believe it is either the Maréchal de Saint André, the Duc de Nemours, or the Chevalier de Guise whom I must envy.

She blushed deeply and said, I shall not answer that question or say anything which might increase or decrease your suspicions, and if you try to find out by watching my behavior I shall become so nervous that in the end everybody will notice. For God's sake, therefore, arrange, under some pretext of illness, that I see nobody.

No, Madame, it would soon be known that it was a sham, and furthermore I want to put my trust in you

alone; both my heart and my reason approve of this course. In your present state of mind I have you under closer guard by giving you your liberty than in any other way I could imagine.

M. de Clèves was not mistaken. The perfect trust he put in his wife strengthened her defenses against M. de Nemours and made her more strict in her resolutions than any restraint of his could possibly have done. So she went about her ordinary business at the Louvre and with the Queen-Dauphine, and avoided the company and the looks of M. de Nemours so assiduously that she almost killed the joy he had felt at thinking himself loved by her; indeed her every action now persuaded him that she did not. He even began to wonder whether he had not dreamt the whole thing, so unlikely did it seem. Madame de Clèves, however, could not conceal her terrible unhappiness, and this reassured him; all the charm in the world could not have increased his love so much as this austere behavior.

One evening, when M. and Madame de Clèves were with the Queen somebody mentioned a rumor that the King was appointing one more great noble of the Court to accompany Madame to Spain, and added that it would probably be either the Maréchal de Saint André or the Chevalier de Guise. M. de Clèves' eyes were upon his wife as these names were mentioned, and he saw that she was quite unaffected by them and by the idea that they would be on the journey with her. This made him think that it was neither of them whose presence she

dreaded, and wanting to clear up his suspicions he went to the Queen's closet where the King was. He stayed there a little while, and then returned to his wife and whispered in her ear that he had just learned it was M. de Nemours who would go with them.

This name, and the thought that she would be obliged to see him every day of a long journey, in the presence of her husband, threw Madame de Clèves into a state of agitation that she could not conceal, and wishing to put it onto something else she said,

I think the choice of this Prince is a very bad one from your point of view, as he will have equal honors with you. You ought to try and arrange for some other person to go, not him.

This fear of M. de Nemours coming with me has nothing to do with honors, Madame, said M. de Clèves. You mind it for a different reason, and your dejection has shown me something that with any other woman I should have learnt from her joy. Have no fear, however; what I have just told you is not true—I invented it to confirm my suspicions.

On these words he left the room. He could see that his wife was deeply embarrassed and had no wish to add to her embarrassment by his presence. At that moment M. de Nemours arrived and saw at once the state Madame de Clèves was in. He went up to her and said his regard for her forbade him to ask why she was so far away, even more than usual. M. de Nemours' voice brought her back to earth, though she did not take in

the sense of what he said. Full as she was of her own thoughts, terrified that her husband might see him with her, she said, Oh! For God's sake let me be!

Alas, Madame, he replied, I do nothing but let you be; what is your complaint? I do not dare speak with you, hardly even to look at you; I tremble to go near you. Do I deserve that you should speak to me like this? And why do you imply that your grief has something to do with me?

Madame de Clèves was very angry with herself for having given M. de Nemours an opening to speak plainly as never before. She left him without another word and went back to her own room more agitated than she had ever been. Her husband realized this the moment he saw her; he also realized that she dreaded his speaking of what had happened. He followed her into a little room saying, Don't avoid me; I will say nothing that could displease you. I want you to forgive me for startling you just now—I am punished enough for it by what I found out. Of all men M. de Nemours is the one I was most afraid of, and I see your danger. You must control yourself for your own sake and, if possible, for love of me—I don't ask it as a husband, merely as a man whose happiness depends on you and who loves you even more tenderly and passionately than you love that other.

As he spoke, M. de Clèves broke down and could hardly finish what he was saying. His wife was penetrated to the heart, and bursting into tears she embraced him with such tender sorrow that his mood changed a

little. They stayed like this a while and separated without having spoken again; indeed they had no more strength for words.

Everything was now ready for the wedding of Madame. The Duke of Alba arrived to marry her and was given a magnificent reception with all the ceremonies proper to such an occasion. To meet him the King sent the Prince de Condé, the Cardinals of Lorraine and Guise, the Dukes of Lorraine, Ferrara, Aumale, Bouillon, Guise and Nemours, accompanied by gentlemen and pages dressed in their liveries. The King himself awaited the Duke of Alba at the first gate of the Louvre with two hundred gentlemen in waiting, headed by the Constable. When the Duke came up to the King he would have embraced his knees, but the King prevented him, making him walk at his side to the Queen's apartment and then to Madame's, to whom the Duke of Alba gave a magnificent present on behalf of his master. Next he went to Madame Marguerite, the King's sister, and said many complimentary things about the Duke of Savoy, assuring her that he would be there in a very few days.

Parties were given at the Louvre to show all the Court beauties to the Duke of Alba and the Prince of Orange, who accompanied him, and Madame de Clèves did not dare stay away, however much she may have wished to do so, for fear of displeasing her husband who absolutely ordered her to go to them. What decided her to do so even more than this was the absence of M. de Nemours, who had gone to meet the Duke of Savoy and who, even

after the arrival of this prince, was obliged to be with him all the time helping him with everything to do with the wedding ceremonies. So Madame de Clèves saw him much less than usual, and this gave her some degree of tranquillity.

THE Vidame de Chartres had by no means forgotten his conversation with M. de Nemours. He felt sure that the story which the Prince had told him was his own and he watched him so carefully that he would very likely have discovered the truth had not the arrival of the Dukes of Alba and Savoy produced a new bustle in the life at Court which prevented him from seeing what otherwise could have enlightened him. His curiosity, as well as a natural inclination to tell everything to the person one loves, made him tell Madame de Martigues about the extraordinary action of the lady who had confessed her passion for another man to her own husband. He assured her that it was undoubtedly M. de Nemours who had inspired this passion and begged her to help him keep this Prince under observation. Madame de Martigues was enchanted with what the Vidame told her; she had always noticed that the Queen-Dauphine was very curious about everything to do with M. de Nemours, and this made her more anxious than ever to find out the truth of the story.

A few days before that which had been chosen for the wedding the Queen-Dauphine gave a supper party for her father-in-law the King and the Duchesse de Valentinois. Madame de Clèves, who had been busy dressing, went to the Louvre later than usual and on the way she met a gentleman from the Queen-Dauphine coming to fetch

her. When she arrived in her room the Princess called to her from the bed, where she lay, that she had been waiting impatiently for her.

Madame de Clèves said, I am not sure that I am going to be grateful for this eagerness. Does it really come from a wish to see me or something else?

Quite right, said the Queen-Dauphine, but all the same you should be grateful because I've got a story for you which I know you'll find fascinating.

Madame de Clèves knelt by the bed, and fortunately for her the light did not fall on her face.

You know, said this Queen, how we have been dying to guess what has made the Duc de Nemours so different. I believe I know it now, and it's something that will amaze you. He is madly in love with one of the beauties here at the Court and she loves him too.

It is easy to imagine the pang these words gave to Madame de Clèves; she could not think that they applied to her, since, as far as she knew, nobody had any idea that she loved M. de Nemours.

This doesn't seem very extraordinary to me, she said, considering M. de Nemours' age and how handsome he is.

That's not the surprise, said Madame la Dauphine. Listen. This woman who loves M. de Nemours has never given him any reason to suppose that she does, and furthermore, she is so much afraid that she will not always be able to control her passion that she has told her husband everything so that he shall take her away from

the Court. And all this comes straight from M. de Nemours himself.

If Madame de Clèves had begun by feeling hurt that she was not involved in this gossip, Madame la Dauphine's last words involved her a good deal too much and she was plunged into despair by them. She could not speak, and remained with her forehead leaning against the bed while the Queen prattled on, so much absorbed in what she was saying that she paid no attention to this embarrassment. When Madame de Clèves had recovered herself she said, I don't think all this sounds very probable, Madame, and I should like to know who told it to you?

Madame de Martigues told me and she got it from the Vidame de Chartres—you know he is in love with her. The Duc de Nemours himself told him, though not the name of the lady, nor did he admit to being the man she loved, but the Vidame doesn't doubt for a moment that he is.

As Madame la Dauphine finished speaking somebody came up to the bed. Madame de Clèves was in such a position that she could not see who it was, but she soon guessed when Madame la Dauphine, with a look of cheerful surprise, cried out, Here's the very person! Now I'm going to ask him all about it.

So Madame de Clèves realized that the newcomer was the Duc de Nemours. Without turning towards him she threw herself upon Madame la Dauphine and whispered that on no account must she speak to him about this story which he had confided in the Vidame de Chartres

or she might cause a quarrel between them. But the Queen-Dauphine only laughed at her, saying she was too cautious, and turned back to M. de Nemours, who was already dressed for the party. He said, in his usual charming way, It seems to me, Madame, if I might hazard a guess, that you were talking about me when I came in, that you were going to ask me something and that Madame de Clèves was trying to stop you.

Quite right, said Madame la Dauphine, but I am not going to give in to her this time. I want you to tell me if a certain story I heard is true, and if you are not the man who loves and is loved by a lady of the Court who carefully keeps her feelings from you but has confessed them to her husband.

If death could have come at this moment to rescue Madame de Clèves from her embarrassment she would have welcomed it, and as for M. de Nemours he was even more embarrassed, if possible. That Madame la Dauphine, who, he believed, did not hate him, should speak like this in front of Madame de Clèves, her greatest friend, whom she trusted and who trusted her completely, put so many curious ideas into his head that he really could not control his expression. He saw that Madame de Clèves had been put into a terrible situation, and all through his fault; he thought that now he had done something for which she must hate him. He was thunderstruck and speechless.

Madame la Dauphine, seeing that he was fearfully taken aback, said to Madame de Clèves, Just look at him and see if it's not his own story.

138

However M. de Nemours, recovering from the first shock and seeing the necessity of doing something quickly which would get them out of this dangerous situation, mastered himself all of a sudden and said, I must confess, Madame, to a good deal of surprise and distress that the Vidame de Chartres should have been so disloyal as to talk about my friend's affairs, which I had told him as a secret. I could have my revenge, he went on, calmly smiling in a way that almost lulled the suspicions of Madame la Dauphine. He has confided various things in me which are by no means unimportant to him. But, Madame, he went on, I wonder why you do me the honor of laying all this at my door? The Vidame can hardly have said that I was involved since I had told him precisely the contrary. Perhaps the role of a lover might suit me, but that of a beloved—well, Madame, I should have thought you, of all people, would know better.

The Prince was glad of an opportunity to refer to the past, to a time when he had given the Queen-Dauphine a certain understanding, hoping that like this he would change her ideas. She knew what he meant, or thought she did, but without answering she continued to make sport of his embarrassment.

I have been very uneasy, he went on, over my friend, his interests and the well deserved reproaches he will make me for having spoken of something which to him is dearer than life itself. All the same he did not tell me everything, and I don't know the name of the woman

he loves; all I know is that nobody is more in love, or more to be pitied.

Why so much to be pitied, said Madame la Dauphine, if he is loved in return?

But do you think he is loved, Madame? Do you think that a woman who was really in love would ever have told her husband? It must be somebody who does not know what love is; she probably felt a sort of gratitude for the passion she had inspired. I don't think my friend can flatter himself that there is much hope for him, but all the same, poor creature, he is happy to think that at least he made her fear that she might love him and he would not change places with the luckiest lover in all the world.

Your friend and his passion are easily satisfied, said Madame la Dauphine, and I am beginning to think you are not telling about yourself; indeed it wouldn't take much to make me think, like Madame de Clèves, that none of this can ever have happened.

No, I really don't think it can have, remarked Madame de Clèves, who so far had not said a word, and if it had, how should we know it? It's not very likely that the sort of woman who could do such an extraordinary thing would be foolish enough to go telling people, and you wouldn't expect the husband to, either—if he did he would be most unworthy of his wife's action.

M. de Nemours, seeing that Madame de Clèves suspected her husband, was only too pleased to increase her suspicions; he knew quite well that this rival was going to be the most difficult to eradicate. Ah, he said, a hus-

band can commit many imprudences through jealousy, or a wish, perhaps, to find out more than he has been told.

Madame de Clèves was now at the end of her strength and her courage and, unable to bear this conversation any longer, she was just going to say that she felt ill when, luckily for her, the Duchesse de Valentinois arrived and told the Queen-Dauphine that the King was coming. The Queen-Dauphine went into her dressing room to get ready and as Madame de Clèves was about to follow her M. de Nemours came up and said, I would give my life to have a word with you, but of all the many important things I want to say, the most urgent is this: I beg you to believe that if I said anything which the Dauphine might take to herself I did so for reasons far removed from her.

Madame de Clèves pretended not to have heard; she left M. de Nemours without so much as a glance and followed the King who had just appeared. There were a great many people with him. She got caught up in her train, slipped and fell, and then made this accident an excuse to leave. She pretended that she could not go on, and went home, and in truth she was not equal to staying there.

M. de Clèves came to the Louvre and was surprised not to find his wife until they told him of her accident. He went home at once to see how she was, found her in bed and learnt that there was nothing much wrong with her. He had not been with her for long before he realized

that she was feeling desperately sad and he wondered why.

What's the matter? he said. You seem to have something besides the pain that you speak of?

I am terribly worried and unhappy, she replied. How have you repaid the trust I put in you, mad as I must have been? Surely I deserved that you should keep the secret and even if I did not deserve it, was it not in your own interest to have kept it? Curiosity to know the name I could not tell drove you, I suppose, to this cruel piece of recklessness. Was it necessary to be so curious? I may tell you that the results could hardly be more grievous. The whole story has come out; people have just been telling it, without knowing that it has such a special interest for me.

What is this, Madame—you accuse me of having repeated something that passed between you and me, you tell me that all is known! I am not going to justify myself—you would not believe me if I did—but of course you must have taken somebody else's story for your own.

But there could not be another story like mine; no other woman would be capable of such a thing! Nobody could have invented or imagined it; nobody but me has ever conceived of such a thing. Madame la Dauphine has just told it to me word for word; she got it from the Vidame de Chartres and he from M. de Nemours.

M. de Nemours! cried M. de Clèves, with a despairing gesture. So, M. de Nemours knows that you love him and that I know it.

You always pick on M. de Nemours, she replied, and I tell you again that I am not going to make any remark upon your suspicions. I have no idea whether M. de Nemours knows that I figure in this story or that you have allotted him the other character; be that as it may, he told it to the Vidame de Chartres, saying that it had happened to a friend of his who had kept back the lady's name. I suppose this friend of M. de Nemours is also a friend of yours, and that you put yourself in his hands in the hopes of being enlightened.

Is there a friend in all the world to whom one would make such a confidence, said M. de Clèves. It would be a heavy price to pay for enlightenment, to tell a thing one is trying to hide, even from oneself. I think, Madame, that it is rather for you to ask yourself whom you have told, since the secret is more likely to have got out through you than through me. Your difficulties became too much for you, you could no longer bear them alone, and you sought relief in wailing to some confidante who has betrayed you.

You want to crush me to earth, she cried, by accusing me of something you yourself have done, and it is very cruel of you. How can you suspect me? I was brave enough to speak to you; how can you think I would breathe a word to anybody else?

Indeed Madame de Clèves, by the confession to her husband, had given such absolute proof of sincerity, and she denied having told anybody else with such vehemence, that M. de Clèves hardly knew what to think. He knew that he had not told anybody and yet

143

a thing which could not possibly be guessed at was now known, and could only be known through one or the other of them. But to him what mattered most was that somebody was now in possession of this secret, and that soon it must become common knowledge.

These selfsame thoughts were also passing through the mind of Madame de Clèves. She found it equally impossible to believe that her husband had, or had not, talked, though M. de Nemours' words about curiosity making the indiscretion of husbands seemed so directly related to M. de Clèves' state of mind that she could hardly believe it was said by accident and they made her think that M. de Clèves must have abused her trust in him. They were both so much absorbed that they remained a long while without saying a word, only coming out of this silence to repeat what had already been said several times; finally they were more estranged in heart and soul than they had ever been.

It is not difficult to imagine what sort of a night each of them spent. M. de Clèves' reserves of fortitude were already exhausted by his efforts to endure the agonizing spectacle of his adored wife in love with somebody else. He could bear it no more, and indeed felt that he ought not to bear something so prejudicial to his good name. He no longer knew what to think of his wife. He no longer knew what he ought to make her do or how he himself ought to behave; on every hand he saw some deadly peril. Finally, after much painful indecision, he made up his mind, in view of the Spanish journey, to do nothing which could draw attention to his unhappy state.

He went to find Madame de Clèves, and told her that it was no longer a question of finding out which of them had given away the secret but of making it quite obvious that the story was a fable and nothing to do with her, and that he relied on her to persuade M. de Nemours and the others of this, which she could do by treating him with all the coldness and strictness due to a man who was letting her see that he loved her.

Like this she would easily disabuse him of the idea that she had a fancy for him; there was no point in worrying about what he might be thinking because, so long as she did not weaken, these thoughts would disappear of their own accord. Above all, he said, it was absolutely essential for her to go in the ordinary way to the Louvre and to all the parties.

On this, M. de Clèves left his wife without waiting for an answer.

She thought there was a great deal in what he said, and that her anger with M. de Nemours would make it quite easy for her to carry out his wishes, though she knew it would not be easy to look happy and carefree at the wedding ceremonies. Since, however, she had been chosen from among many ladies to carry the Dauphine's train she could hardly have got out of doing so without causing a great deal of gossip and curiosity as to what her reason might be. So she made up her mind to a tremendous effort, and, taking the whole of that day to prepare for it, she retired alone to her closet and gave herself over to her worries. What seemed to her the worst feature of the whole affair was that she now had this cause

:r against M. de Nemours, for whom, try as she might, she could find no justification. She could not doubt that he had told the story to the Vidame de Chartres—he had owned as much—neither could she doubt, from the way in which he had spoken, that he knew it had to do with her. How could she forgive such an indiscretion? And what could have come over this Prince, whose discretion hitherto had so touched her heart? She said to herself, He was discreet enough while he thought he had nothing to hope for, but the mere hint of success, even if very uncertain, quite changed his outlook. As soon as he thought himself beloved he wanted everybody to know it and said as much as he could. I never admitted to loving him; he guessed it, and let it be seen that he had guessed. Had he been certain he would have acted differently. How mistaken I was when I thought he would have the strength to hide anything which flattered his own vanity! And it is for the sake of this man, who seemed to me so different, that I find myself on a level with other women, I, who used to be different indeed; I have thrown away the love and esteem of a husband who should have made my joy, and soon everybody will know that I am the victim of a wild and uncontrollable passion—M. de Nemours knows it already. Yet it was in order to avoid these very misfortunes that I risked my peace of mind, perhaps even life itself.

These sad thoughts called forth a torrent of tears; but in her heart she knew quite well that she could have

146

borne anything had she been satisfied with M. de Nemours' behavior.

This Prince, on his side, was in no better case. The thought of his indiscretion in having spoken to the Vidame of Chartres, and its cruel consequences, tormented him; he could hardly bear to think of the embarrassment and misery he had seen on Madame de Clèves' face, and was inconsolable at some of the things he had said to her about this affair which, though they may have been romantic in themselves, seemed to him now both brutal and indiscreet, taking for granted that she knew that she was the lady in love and that he was the object of that love. He only longed to speak with her, though feeling that he ought to dread this rather than wish for it.

What could I say to her? Underline what I have already said too definitely? Force her to see that I know she loves me—I who have never even dared to tell her of my love? Should I begin by speaking openly about my passion for her like a man driven to taking liberties by his longing? How can I even think of approaching her? The very sight of me must embarrass her now. I cannot justify myself. I have no excuse. I am quite simply unworthy that she should look at me and I cannot hope that she ever will again. She sought a defense against me, and might never have found one had I myself not put it into her hands. I have thrown away the distinction and happiness of being loved by this good and lovely woman. I would not even have minded that so much had I not dealt her such a blow at the same time. It is for the

harm I have done her that I am suffering, even more than for that I have done myself in her eyes.

These thoughts went round and round in M. de Nemours' brain; he was tormented by them, and all the time he was longing to speak with Madame de Clèves. He considered how he could manage this: he thought of writing to her, but at last decided that, having put himself in the wrong, and taking her present mood into account, the best would be to show his deep respect by keeping a sorrowful silence, to let her see that he did not dare to approach her, and to trust that time, luck, and her inclination would do something for him.

Madame's betrothal took place the next day, and her wedding the day after that, and these ceremonies kept the whole Court so busy that it was not difficult for Madame de Clèves and M. de Nemours to conceal their agitation. Madame la Dauphine hardly mentioned the conversation with M. de Nemours to Madame de Clèves, and M. de Clèves only spoke to her of current events, so that she was not nearly as much embarrassed as she had expected to be.

The engagement took place at the Louvre, and after a banquet and a ball the whole of the royal household went to sleep, as was the custom, at Evêché, a royal residence near the Louvre. Next morning the Duke of Alba, who usually dressed with great simplicity, wore a coat of cloth of gold shot with flame, yellow and black, all embroidered with precious stones, and on his head a closed crown. The Prince of Orange, magnificent, followed by the servants in his livery and all the other

Spaniards followed by theirs, came for the Duke of Alba at the Hôtel de Villeroi where he was staying, and then all advanced upon Evêché, marching in fours. As soon as he had arrived there was a procession to the Church, the King leading Madame, who also had a closed crown. Her train was carried by Mesdemoiselles de Montpensier and Longueville The Queen came next, without a crown, and after her the Queen-Dauphine, Madame the King's sister, Madame de Lorraine and the Queen of Navarre, all of whom had their trains carried by Princesses. The attendants of the Queens and the Princesses were magnificently dressed in the same colors as themselves, so that one could see which their ladies were by the colors of their gowns. A platform had been specially built inside the Church; they all mounted onto this and the marriage ceremonies were then performed. Afterwards they dined at Evêché, leaving at about five o'clock to go to the palace where a banquet was given for members of the parliament, the royal households and dignitaries of the town. The King, the Queens, the Princes and Princesses ate from the marble table in the great hall of the palace, the Duke of Alba sitting next the new Queen of Spain. A step below the marble table, on the King's right hand, was a table for ambassadors, archbishops and knights of the various orders, while on the other side was a table for members of the parliament.

The Duc de Guise, dressed in gold frieze, served the King as Great Chamberlain, M. le Prince de Condé as Steward of the Household, and the Duc de Nemours as Cupbearer. When the tables had been removed the ball

began, with interludes consisting of ballets and wonder-
ful theatrical machinery. Finally, after midnight, the
King and the whole Court went back to the Louvre. Sad
though Madame de Clèves might have been feeling, her
beauty was unaffected; in the eyes of the world and above
all in those of M. de Nemours it seemed incomparable.
He did not venture to speak to her, though he could
easily have done so during the ceremonies, but let her
see how subdued he was and how respectfully aloof—so
much so that she began to think him less to blame al-
though he had not said anything which could justify his
behavior. For the next few days his conduct was the same
and it made the same impression upon Madame de
Clèves.

At last the day of the tournament arrived. The Queens
went to their places in the galleries and on the platforms
specially built for them.

The four champions appeared at the ends of the lists,
with a great number of horses and men in livery—the
most magnificent sight that has ever been seen in France.

The King always had the same colors—white and
black, which he wore in honor of Madame de Valen-
tinois, who was a widow. The Duke of Ferrara and his
retinue were in yellow and red. M. de Guise appeared in
carnation and white and everybody wondered why he
had chosen these colors until it was remembered that
they were those of a certain beauty he had loved before
her marriage, and whom he still loved though he no
longer dared allow her to see it. M. de Nemours had
yellow and black and the reason for this was sought in

Was it for Respect?

vain by all but Madame de Clèves, who guessed it without difficulty, remembering that she had once said in front of him that she loved yellow and was sorry that being so fair it did not suit her. The Prince therefore felt he could take it without indiscretion; Madame de Clèves never wore it and nobody could think that it was her color.

The champions now performed unheard-of prodigies of skill; the King was the best horseman in the land, yet it was difficult to choose between them. M. de Nemours was so graceful in all his gestures that it did not need the special interest felt by Madame de Clèves to be very much inclined in his favor. As soon as she saw him appear at the end of the lists she felt an extraordinary emotion, and she could scarcely conceal her joy each time he won a heat. Towards evening, when it was nearly over and everybody was getting ready to go home, the King, most unluckily for his country, decided to break one more lance. He sent for the Comte de Montgoméry, who was very skilled, to come into the lists. The Count begged the King to be let off, making all the excuses he could think of, but the King, almost angrily, insisted.

Then the Queen sent a message to the King begging him to give over, to be content with his great success and come and join her.

He replied that it was in her honor that he was going to fight once more, and entered the ring. She sent the Duke of Savoy to beg him a second time, but to no avail. He fought, the lances were shattered, and a splinter

from that of M. de Montgoméry lodged in his eye. The Prince fell from his horse; his equerries and M. de Montmorency, one of the marshals, ran to him, thunderstruck to see him wounded. But the King was perfectly calm, saying that it was very slight and that he forgave the Comte de Montgoméry. So this day, which was to have been so delightful, ended in a dire calamity causing an agitation and sorrow which can easily be imagined.

As soon as the King had been put to bed the surgeons who examined his wound pronounced it to be very serious, and now the Constable remembered the prophecy which had been made to the King that he would be killed in single combat, and he felt sure that this prophecy was about to be fulfilled. The King of Spain, who was at Brussels, was informed of the accident and immediately sent his own doctor, a man of great reputation, but he considered that there was no hope for the King.

A Court divided as this one was and full of opposing interests would naturally be thrown into a fever of agitation on the eve of so momentous an event; nevertheless all the intrigues went on behind closed doors and apparently there was only one absorbing preoccupation— the King's health. The Queens, the Princes and Princesses hardly left his antechamber.

Madame de Clèves was supposed to be there too. But so, she knew, would M. de Nemours and then she would never be able to hide her embarrassment from the eyes of her husband; she realized too, that the mere sight of this Prince made her feel that he had been in the right and melted her resolutions. She therefore pretended to be

ill. The Court had other things to think of than her behavior and whether she was really ill or not; her husband was the only person who knew the truth, and she did not mind him knowing it. So she remained at home, indifferent to the great change there was going to be and free to think at leisure of her own affairs.

Everybody was with the King. M. de Clèves came back from time to time with the latest bulletin. He was exactly the same as he had always been with her except that when they were alone together he was a little colder and more reserved. He never spoke of what had passed between them and she, even had she thought it wise, did not feel strong enough to broach the subject.

M. de Nemours, who had expected a chance of speaking with Madame de Clèves, was surprised and upset not even to have the joy of seeing her.

The King's wound was so serious that on the seventh day the doctors gave him up. He showed great fortitude in the face of death, all the more creditable considering that he was losing his life through a miserable accident, dying in the flower of his youth, happy, adored by his people, and loved by a mistress with whom he was madly in love. On the eve of his death he married Madame, his sister, to the Duke of Savoy without any ceremony.

The Duchesse de Valentinois' state of mind can be imagined. The Queen would not allow her to see the King, and sent to her for his seals and the crown jewels which she always kept. The Duchess asked whether the King were dead, and on being told that he was not she

said, In that case I own no other master and nobody can make me give up what he confided to me.

As soon as he had expired, at the Château de Tournelles, the Dukes of Ferrara, Guise and Nemours conducted the Queen-Mother, the new King, and the Queen, his wife, to the Louvre. The Queen-Mother was led by M. de Nemours. As they started she went back a few steps and told her daughter-in-law the Queen that now it was her place to go first, but it was easy to see that these fair words were spoken in no spirit of goodwill.

THE Cardinal de Lorraine's influence with the Queen was now paramount and the Vidame de Chartres was quite out of favor. He did not mind this as much as he ought to have, finding consolation in his love for Madame de Martigues and love of liberty. The Cardinal had plenty of time, during the ten days of the King's illness, to lay his schemes and to make the Queen take decisions which would further them. Thus, as soon as the King was dead, the Queen ordered the Constable to remain with his body, at Tournelles, for the usual ceremonies, a task which separated him from all that was going on and took away all liberty of action. He sent a messenger to the King of Navarre urging him to come with all speed so that together they might make a stand against great acquisition of power by the Guise brothers.

The Duc de Guise was given command of the army and the Cardinal de Lorraine put in charge of finance. The Duchesse de Valentinois was driven away from the Court, and the Cardinal de Tournon, an open enemy of the Constable, was recalled, as was the Chancelier Olivier, open enemy of the Duchesse de Valentinois; in short the whole aspect of the Court was changed. The Duc de Guise carried the King's mantle during the funeral ceremonies exactly as if he had been a Prince of the Blood, and he and his brothers ruled supreme, not only because of the Cardinal's influence over the Queen

but because this Princess supposed that she would be able to get rid of them if they displeased her, which she could never have done with the Constable, supported as he was by Princes of the Blood.

When the mourning ceremonies were over the Constable went to the Louvre and was received with a good deal of coldness by the new King. He had hoped to see him alone, but the King sent for the Guises and said, in front of them, that he advised him to take a rest, that the army and finances had been disposed of and that he would send for him if he ever needed him. The Queen-Mother received him even more coldly than the King, and even reproached him for having told the late King that his children did not look like him.

The King of Navarre arrived and his reception was no better. The Prince de Condé, who had less self-control than his brother, complained to everybody—to no avail however; he was simply removed from the Court and sent to Flanders to sign the ratification of the peace treaty. The King of Navarre was shown a forged letter, purporting to come from the King of Spain, accusing him of having designs on his territory; it was suggested to him that his land was in danger and that he had better go back to Béarn. The Queen provided him with the means of doing so, putting Madame Elizabeth in his charge and even making him go ahead of this Princess. Thus there was not a single person left at the Court who could balance the power of the House of Guise.

Although M. de Clèves was annoyed at not going with Madame Elizabeth, he could not say anything in view of

the importance of the substitute, and indeed it was not so much for the honors which the mission would have brought that he regretted it as the fact that it would have been a way for his wife to leave the Court without looking as if she wanted to.

A few days after the King's death it was decided to go to Rheims for the Coronation. As soon as this journey was mooted, Madame de Clèves, who still kept to her room, pretended to be ill and begged her husband to let her off from following the Court and to allow her to go, for a change of air, to Coulommiers. He replied that he had no wish to find out whether it was really her health which prevented her from going to Rheims, but that in any case he gave his consent. It was no trouble to him; he had already come to the same decision. Highly though he rated his wife's virtue, he saw that it would not be prudent to expose it any longer to the sight of the man she loved.

M. de Nemours soon found out that Madame de Clèves was not going with the Court, and, unable to bear going without having seen her, he went to call on the eve of his departure, as late as he decently could, in the hopes of finding her alone. Luck was with him. As he came into the courtyard he found Madame de Nevers and Madame de Martigues who were just leaving and who told him that they had left her alone. He went upstairs in a state of agitation which was nothing compared with that of Madame de Clèves when they told her that M. de Nemours was there to see her.

Fear that he might speak of his passion, fear of giving too favorable a reply, of the anxiety this visit would cause

her husband, of giving an account of it to her husband or of hiding it from him, all these fears assailed her and threw her into such a fever of embarrassment that she resolved to avoid the one thing she longed for most in the world. She sent one of her maids to M. de Nemours, who was in her antechamber, to say that she had been taken ill and regretted that she must decline the honor he wished to do her. What sorrow for this Prince, not only not to have seen Madame de Clèves but that this should have been so by her own wish! He left the next day feeling that there was now nothing to hope for; he had not spoken to her since the conversation with Madame la Dauphine and he had reason to suppose that he had ruined his own chances of success by what he had told the Vidame. His pain was deeply tinged with bitterness.

As soon as Madame de Clèves had recovered from her first emotion at the idea of a visit from the Duke, all the reasons for not seeing him melted away and she even thought she had been in the wrong. Had she dared to do so, had there still been time, she would have had him called back.

Meanwhile Mesdames de Nevers and Martigues went on to the Queen-Dauphine and there they found M. de Clèves. This Princess asked where they had been and they said they had just come from Madame de Clèves' where they had spent the afternoon with quite a lot of people but that only M. de Nemours was there when they left.

These words which seemed harmless to them, were not so to M. de Clèves. Although he must have realized that M. de Nemours had numerous opportunities of speaking

with his wife, the idea of him alone with her, able to tell her of his love, suddenly came upon him with all the force of novelty, and he was more violently jealous than he had ever been. He could not stay at the Queen's and went home hardly knowing why he went or whether he intended to interrupt M. de Nemours. When he came to his house he looked for signs that M. de Nemours was still there, was relieved to see that he was not, and comforted to think that he could not have stayed very long.

Then he imagined that perhaps it was not of M. de Nemours that he ought to be jealous, and although he had no real doubts he tried to make himself doubt it, but so many things pointed to him that this mood of wilful indecision did not last long. He went straight to his wife's room, and after having spoken awhile on indifferent subjects he could not resist asking what she had done and whom she had seen, and she gave him an account of everything. When she did not mention M. de Nemours he asked her, trembling with emotion, if that was everybody she had seen, so as to give her the opportunity to name this Prince and thus spare him the sorrow of feeling that she was not being quite frank with him. As she had not seen him she did not name him. M. de Clèves then spoke in a voice which betrayed his anguish. And what about M. de Nemours? Have you not seen him? Perhaps you have forgotten?

No, she replied, I didn't see him. I suddenly felt unwell and sent him one of my maids to make my excuses.

You only feel ill for him, said M. de Clèves. You see everybody else. Why this special behavior for M. de Ne-

-------- .Thy is he not the same as the others? Why let him see that he frightens you, making use of the power his love gives you over him? Would you dare refuse to see him if he did not know quite well that there is more than mere incivility behind your refusal? Why must you be so severe with him? From somebody like you every-thing counts as a favor except indifference.

I never thought, suspicious though you may be of M. de Nemours, that you could reproach me with not having seen him, said Madame de Clèves.

Yes, I do reproach you, and with reason. Why refuse to see him if he has never said anything to you? The answer is that he has spoken; if his silence had been sole witness to his passion it could never have affected you so deeply. You have not been able to tell me the whole truth; you have hidden the greater part of it from me, repenting even of the little you did tell and having no strength to go on. I am more wretched than I thought —the most wretched of all men. You are my wife, I love you like a mistress and I know you are in love with the most fascinating man at Court, who sees you every day and is aware that you love him—I must have been mad to think that you would be able to overcome your passion for him.

Madame de Clèves replied sadly, I do not know whether you were wrong when you approved of my confession, but I cannot help wondering whether I was right in thinking that you would treat me with fairness.

Then stop wondering, he answered, because I can tell you. You were not right. What you expected from me

was as impossible as what I expected from you. How could you hope that I should be reasonable? I suppose you forget that I love you madly and that I am your husband? I might bear anything were it one or the other, but both together make it impossible. Alas, how else do they affect me? I have violent and wavering emotions which I cannot control—I feel myself no longer worthy of you, and you no longer worthy of me. I adore and hate you. I offend you and ask your forgiveness. I admire you and am ashamed to do so. There is no peace in me nor any reason either. I don't know how I have survived the words you spoke at Coulommiers, or the day you heard from Madame la Dauphine that your story was public property. I have no means of guessing how it came out, or what may have passed on the subject between yourself and M. de Nemours—you will never explain this, nor do I ask that you should; I only ask you to bear in mind that you have made me the unhappiest man in the world.

On these words M. de Clèves left his wife's room, and went off the next day without seeing her again, but he wrote her a letter full of goodness and affection. Her reply was so touching, so reassuring as to her past and future conduct, that, since all this was founded upon truth and she really meant what she wrote, it made a great impression upon M. de Clèves. He felt more easy in his mind, especially as M. de Nemours was also with the King, and no longer in the same place as Madame de Clèves. Whenever this Princess spoke with her husband, his love for her, her candid behavior, her friendship for

him and her duty towards him were enough to drive the image of M. de Nemours out of his heart. But these impressions only lasted a little while and then he reverted to his original idea which was becoming more and more real to him.

For a day or two after the Duc de Nemours had left the Court Madame de Clèves hardly noticed his absence. Soon, however, she began to feel it cruelly. Since the beginning of her love for him not a day had passed but she could look for a meeting with alternate longing and apprehension, and she suffered to think that chance could no longer bring them face to face. She went to Coulommiers, taking with her two big pictures which had been copied for her from originals painted for Madame de Valentinois' beautiful house at Anet and which represented all the outstanding events of the King's reign. Among others there was the siege of Metz, with portraits of all those who had distinguished themselves there; M. de Nemours was one of these and perhaps that may have been the reason why Madame de Clèves was so anxious to own these paintings.

Madame de Martigues, who was unable to leave with the Court, promised her to spend a few days at Coulommiers. The fact that they were both in such favor with the Queen had never caused any jealousy between them and they were friends, though they did not confide all their emotions to each other. Madame de Clèves knew that Madame de Martigues loved the Vidame but Madame de Martigues did not know that Madame de Clèves loved and was loved by M. de Nemours. Madame de

Clèves, as niece of the Vidame, was doubly dear to Madame de Martigues, and she loved her back, the more so for knowing that she was also somebody with a passion, and that for an intimate friend of her own beloved.

So Madame de Martigues came, as she had promised, to Coulommiers, and there she found her friend leading a very solitary existence; indeed she took special steps to be left quite alone so that she could spend her evenings, without any servants, in the garden.

She would go to the pavilion where M. de Nemours had heard her speak, into the room that opened on the garden, while her women and servants stayed on the other side, only going to her if she called them. Madame de Martigues had never seen Coulommiers and was amazed by its many beauties, above all the charm of this pavilion; she and Madame de Clèves sat there every evening. These two young women, both passionately in love, alone together in such a beautiful spot, could never come to the end of all they had to say and though they made no confidences they took great pleasure in each other's company.

Madame de Martigues would have been sorry to leave Coulommiers had she not been going to a place where she was to find the Vidame. She left for Chambord, where the Court then was.

The Coronation had been celebrated at Rheims, by the Cardinal de Lorraine, and the rest of the summer was to be spent at Chambord, which had just been built. The Queen was very happy to see Madame de Martigues

again and asked her to tell about Madame de Clèves and what she did with herself in the country. M. de Nemours and M. de Clèves were both in the Queen's room at the time. Madame de Martigues, who had thought Coulommiers delightful, told of all its beauties and extended herself in a description of the forest pavilion, describing how Madame de Clèves loved to spend part of the night there alone. M. de Nemours, knowing the spot well enough to understand what she was talking about, thought it not impossible that he could see Madame de Clèves there without her seeing him. He asked Madame de Martigues some questions to make more certain, and M. de Clèves, who had been watching him all the time she was speaking and thought he could guess exactly what was passing through his mind, was confirmed in his thought when he heard these questions. He felt sure that this Prince was planning to go to see his wife, nor was he mistaken. M. de Nemours was so much taken up with the idea that, after thinking all night how it could be put into practice, next morning he asked the King's permission, on some pretext or other which he invented, to take leave and go to Paris.

M. de Clèves had no doubts as to the motive of this departure, and he now decided that he would find out once and for all how his wife behaved, and put an end to the cruel suspense in which he lived. He would have liked to leave at the same time as M. de Nemours, and to see for himself, from some hiding place, whether this journey was successful, but he was afraid that his departure might seem rather odd, and that M. de Nemours,

hearing of it, would change his plans. So he decided to trust one of his gentlemen, upon whose fidelity and good sense he could rely. He told him everything, of his own dilemma and of the virtuous conduct till then of Madame de Clèves, and ordered him to follow M. de Nemours, keep him under observation and see whether he was not bound for Coulommiers and did not go into the garden after nightfall.

The gentleman, who was quite competent to handle an affair of this sort, did so with great precision. He followed M. de Nemours to a village half a league from Coulommiers where the Prince settled down, no doubt, he thought, to wait for the night. The gentleman decided not to stay with him; he pushed on to a spot in the forest where it seemed that M. de Nemours would be likely to pass by. He was perfectly right in all his conjectures. As soon as night fell he heard footsteps, and, though it was very dark, he easily recognized M. de Nemours. He saw him walk round the garden as though listening if anybody were there and seeking a place where he could easily enter it. The fence was high; beyond that there was another to stop people from coming in, and it was quite hard to do so.

However M. de Nemours managed somehow, and once in the garden it was not difficult to discover the whereabouts of Madame de Clèves. He saw lights in the little room—all its windows were wide open—and gliding along by the fence he went up to it in a state of mind which can be imagined, putting himself behind one of the French windows to see what Madame de

Clèves was doing. She was alone and looking so beautiful that he could hardly control his emotion at the sight of her. It was a hot evening and she wore nothing over her head and bosom but her hair, which hung loose; she lay on a day-bed and on a table beside her there were several baskets full of ribbons. She was picking over these ribbons and choosing out certain ones, and M. de Nemours saw that these were of the very colors he had carried at the tournament. And then he saw that she was making knots and bows to go on an unusual malacca cane. This cane had once been his own; he had given it to his sister, from whom Madame de Clèves had taken it without seeming to recognize it as having once been his. She worked away with a grace and a look of pure goodness which reflected the state of her soul. Then, when she had finished, she took a candlestick and went up to a big table which stood before the picture of the siege of Metz in which was a portrait of M. de Nemours. She sat down and gazed at this portrait in a dream of love.

How to express the feelings of M. de Nemours at this moment? What lover can ever have seen, at night, in the most perfect spot imaginable, the person he adored, have seen her without her knowing it and have seen that she was only occupied with things which had to do with himself and the love she kept hidden from him? It passes the bounds of imagination. The Prince was beside himself, so much so that he forgot the precious minutes were ticking away as he stood there looking at Madame de Clèves. When he was a little more himself

again he thought he had better wait to speak to her until she went into the garden—it seemed the safest plan as then she would be further from her women; but then, seeing that she stayed where she was, he decided to go in. Just as he was about to do so however he was seized with misgivings; she might, he thought, be furious with him, and he could not bear the idea that that sweet expression might change to one of anger on his account. He began to think that he had been incredibly foolish, not in having come to see Madame de Clèves, but to have considered for a moment letting her see him. It would clearly be the height of extravagance to take a lady by surprise, in the middle of the night, to whom he had never even made a declaration of love. He also thought there was little hope that she would listen to him, and that, on the contrary, she would very rightly be angry at the dangerous position he was putting her in. His courage failed him, and several times he was on the point of going away without showing himself. Finally, driven by his intense longing to speak with her, and reassured by the hopeful signs he had just seen, he did advance a few steps, but he was so dreadfully agitated that a scarf he was wearing caught in the window and he made a little noise. Madame de Clèves turned her head, and it may have been her obsession with this Prince, or perhaps enough light fell upon him for her to see who it was—in any case, she thought she recognized him, and without a moment's hesitation, without another look towards him, she went back to her women. She came in so terribly upset that, in order to hide the fact,

she pretended to be ill, thinking too that this would give her people something to occupy them and give M. de Nemours more time to escape.

On further reflection, however, she felt sure that she must have made a mistake and that she had only fancied it was M. de Nemours whom she had seen. She knew him to be at Chambord, and it seemed most unlikely that he would attempt anything so dangerous. She longed to go back, through the little room in the garden, and see if anybody were there, and very likely hoped quite as much as she feared to find M. de Nemours; but in the end prudence prevailed and she decided not to risk clearing the matter up. All the same, it was a long time before she could bring herself to leave a spot so near, perhaps, to this Prince and when at last she got back to the house day had nearly dawned.

M. de Nemours had remained in the garden and while lights were still burning he did not despair of seeing Madame de Clèves again, although he felt sure she had recognized him and had gone away in order to avoid him, but when he saw the doors being shut he realized that he had no more to hope for and went to find his horse, quite near to the place where M. de Clèves' gentleman was waiting. The gentleman then followed him back to the village he had come from.

M. de Nemours decided to spend the day there so that he could go back that night to Coulommiers and see whether Madame de Clèves would be cruel enough to run away again, or even to keep herself hidden from him. Although it was a joy to have seen her so deeply

absorbed in thoughts of him, he was very much cast down that her first instinct should have been to escape.

This Prince was now possessed by a terrible and tender passion which gave him no peace. Behind the house where he was hiding there ran a little willow-bordered stream; here he wandered, and, going as far as he could so that nobody should see or hear him, he gave way to transports of love. His heart was so full that he even wept a little, tears which had nothing to do with grief but were really a distillation of love's magic. He passed in review all Madame de Clèves' actions since first he had fallen in love with her, remembering how perfectly correct she had always been, in spite of her love for him. For after all, he said, she does love me—she does love me. There can be no doubt of that; pledges and promises, favors and indulgences could not make me more certain of it than what I have seen with my own eyes. Yet I am treated as if I were loathed; I had hoped that time would be on my side, but no! The defense against me and against herself goes on. If I were not loved I could think how best to make her fall in love, but I do attract her—I am loved, and it is concealed from me. What have I to hope for and what change of luck can there ever be for me? I am loved by this most adorable creature, and if this brings happiness it also brings agony. Beautiful Princess, he cried, show me your true feelings! Show them to me once—but one little moment—and then I can bear your severity for ever more. Only look at me as you looked last night at my portrait—how could you look so sweetly at my portrait and then so cruelly fly

from my presence? What is it? Why do you fear my love? You love me—useless to try and conceal the fact; you have given me absolute proofs, in spite of yourself. Allow me to enjoy this happiness and stop cutting me to the heart. Is it possible that Madame de Clèves loves me and even so I am unhappy? How beautiful she looked in the night! How could I have resisted throwing myself at her feet? If I had done so perhaps I might have stopped her from running away by reassuring her of my deep respect. All the same it is possible that she did not recognize me; perhaps I am torturing myself unnecessarily and it was simply the sight of a man, at so strange an hour, that terrified her.

All day these thoughts turned round in M. de Nemours' head; he could hardly wait for night to fall and as soon as it did he made for Coulommiers. M. de Clèves' gentleman, who had now assumed a disguise to make himself more unobtrusive, followed him to the same spot as the night before and once more saw him enter the garden. The Prince soon realized that Madame de Clèves had not risked his trying to see her again—every door was shut; he went all round the building looking for lights but there was nothing.

Madame de Clèves, guessing that M. de Nemours would probably come back, had stayed in her own room. She feared that another time she might not have the strength to run away and she would not put herself in a position in which she might be unable to keep up the standard of behavior she had set herself.

M. de Nemours, although he had no longer the slight-

170

est hope of seeing her, could not bring himself to leave a place to which she so often came, and spent the whole night in the garden, finding a certain consolation in the sight of objects on which her eyes rested every day. The sun rose before he thought of going away, but at last fear of being discovered obliged him to do so.

He could not bear to leave for good without seeing Madame de Clèves at all so he went to Madame de Mercoeur, who was at her house in the neighborhood. She was extremely surprised to see her brother but he invented a reason for his journey, plausible enough to take her in, and very cleverly got her to suggest, herself, that they should go and call on Madame de Clèves. This plan was executed the very same day, M. de Nemours telling his sister that he would have to part from her at Coulommiers to go back to the King, thinking that he could let her be the first to leave and thus make certain of being able to speak with Madame de Clèves.

When they arrived she was out walking in a great avenue which bordered the garden. The sight of M. de Nemours upset her terribly, and left her in no doubt that it was he whom she had seen two nights before and she felt really angry with him for behaving so rashly.

The Prince saw a certain coldness in her look and it hurt him bitterly. They talked of nothing in particular, but he did so with such wit, and in such obvious admiration of Madame de Clèves that she could not help thawing a little under his charm. As soon as he felt sure of his ground he asked to go to see the pavilion in the forest, speaking of it as the most delicious spot imaginable and

describing it in such detail that Madame de Mercoeur said he must often have been there as he seemed to know it so well. But Madame de Clèves remarked that it was only just finished and she was sure M. de Nemours had never been there.

On the contrary, said M. de Nemours, with a meaningful look in her direction, I was there a short time ago and it is not very flattering that you should already have forgotten seeing me.

Madame de Mercoeur, who was admiring the garden, was not listening to her brother. Madame de Clèves blushed, lowered her eyes and without looking at M. de Nemours she said,

I don't the least remember having seen you there; indeed if you have been there it must have been without my knowledge.

It is quite true that you never invited me, said M. de Nemours. All the same there I was, and there I experienced the sweetest, cruellest moments I have ever known.

Madame de Clèves understood only too well what he meant, but she said nothing. She wanted to prevent Madame de Mercoeur from going into the little room of the pavilion, not wishing her to see the picture with M. de Nemours in it hanging there, and she managed so well that time went on until Madame de Mercoeur spoke of going home. But when Madame de Clèves realized that M. de Nemours and his sister were not leaving together, she saw what was coming and that she would be in the same embarrassing situation as she had

been once before in Paris, and, as before, was afraid that such a visit would confirm her husband's suspicions. So she took the same line of action, and, in order to avoid being left alone with M. de Nemours, she told Madame de Mercoeur that she would accompany her to the edge of the forest, ordering her own carriage to follow them. The Prince, in despair at seeing that Madame de Clèves still kept up her attitude of terrible strictness, became so pale that Madame de Mercoeur asked him if he felt ill. He threw a look at Madame de Clèves, which nobody else saw, but which plainly told her that what ailed him was simply hope deferred. There was nothing for it but to let them go without following them, and as, after what he had just said, he could hardly have returned with his sister, he went to Paris and spent the night there.

M. de Clèves' gentleman, who had kept him under observation all this time, also went back to Paris; then, seeing M. de Nemours leave for Chambord, he hastened to get there first and give an account of his journey. His master was awaiting his return as though his whole future depended upon it, but as soon as he set eyes upon him he realized, from his look and from his silence, that he had nothing agreeable to tell. The Prince remained a while, his head bowed, speechless with misery, and at last signed to him to go away, saying, I see how it is but I cannot bear to have you tell me.

I have no proof of anything, replied the gentleman, though M. de Nemours did go into the forest garden

two nights running and then the day after went to Coulommiers with Madame de Mercoeur.

Enough, said M. de Clèves, dismissing him with a gesture. That is all I want to know.

The gentleman was obliged to leave his master plunged in utter despair. Seldom can any man with the qualities of heart and mind that distinguished M. de Clèves have suffered the betrayal of wife and mistress at one and the same time. It was too much for him, and he came down that very night with a high fever. He was at once pronounced dangerously ill. Madame de Clèves was sent for and came without delay, to find that he was already much worse. She was amazed and very much upset by the coldness of his manner towards her—he seemed hardly able to bear her to do anything for him; however she thought that this must be a result of his illness.

When she first arrived at Blois, where the Court now was, M. de Nemours could not help feeling very happy to think that she was so near. He tried to see her, going every day to M. de Clèves' room on pretext of hearing how he was, but all in vain. She never left her husband's bedside, and was terribly unhappy about him. M. de Nemours was in despair at her unhappiness, realizing that it would renew her affection for M. de Clèves and that this affection must be a dangerous diversion to the other love in her heart. This thought tormented him for a while, until the extremity of M. de Clèves' illness gave rise to new hopes. He saw that soon Madame de Clèves might be free to follow her own inclinations and that the

future might then open a vista of eternal happiness for him. He was beside himself at this idea, and dared not dwell upon it in case it should come to nothing.

Meanwhile the doctors had all but given up hope. On one of the last days of his illness, the morning after a bad night, M. de Clèves said that he wanted to sleep, and everybody but Madame de Clèves left his room. It seemed to her that he was not only not sleeping, but was exceedingly restless; she went over and knelt by his bed, her face wet with tears. M. de Clèves had made up his mind that she should never know the grievance he had against her, but now he could control himself no more. The loving care that she had showered on him since his illness, her sorrow, which at times he felt to be perfectly genuine and at others the height of hypocrisy, so that he hardly knew what to believe, had thrown him off his balance.

All these tears, he said, are for a death of which you yourself are the cause and which can hardly grieve you as much as you pretend it does. I am in no condition to upbraid you, he went on, his voice extinguished by pain and sorrow, but the fact is that I am dying of sadness because of what you have done. Your courage in speaking to me at Coulommiers has had but a sorry sequel. Why tell me of your passion for M. de Nemours at all if your virtue was not strong enough to resist him? I am ashamed to say my love for you is such that I would far rather have gone on in that state of ignorance out of which you elected to shake me. Why not leave me in my false Paradise?—it is a condition common, I believe, to husbands,

and ı might never have realized, to the end of my life, that you loved M. de Nemours.

Now I am dying, and I should like you to know that, thanks to you, I welcome death. Life would have been odious to me now that I can no longer love and believe in you. Indeed what can life hold for me? The choice between living with her I loved so deeply and who has so cruelly disappointed me, or living apart from her, thus doing violence to my whole nature and to my passionate feelings. I must tell you that these feelings greatly surpassed anything you could have guessed at, since, not wishing to annoy you or to lessen your regard for me by behavior which you might have thought unsuitable in a husband, I kept them hidden from you to a certain extent. I did deserve your love, and as I cannot have it and ought not to wish for it now, I repeat that death means nothing to me. Farewell. Maybe one day you will regret a man whose love for you was just and true—a relationship between two reasonable people—and you will then see a difference between such love as mine and that which merely aims at having the honor to seduce you. But my death will leave you free to make M. de Nemours happy without committing a sin. Not that I should care what happens after I am gone, he added. It is a weakness in me to think of it.

Madame de Clèves, who had no idea at all that her husband had any reason to suspect her, listened to these words without understanding what they could mean, unless they were a reproach for loving M. de Nemours. Suddenly however the scales fell from her eyes.

Committing a sin! she cried. Me? Why such a thought has never entered my head. Virtue herself could not have been more strict than I—I have done nothing behind your back that I would not have done had you been present.

M. de Clèves looked at her with deep contempt and said, Then you would gladly have had me present during those nights you spent with M. de Nemours? I can hardly even now believe it is of you I speak when I speak of a woman spending nights with a man.

But it is not, she cried. I have spent neither nights nor minutes with M. de Nemours—he has never seen me alone—I have never listened to what he had to say—I swear, I swear . . .

M. de Clèves interrupted her, Enough, he said. False vows might hurt me as much as a confession.

Madame de Clèves could not answer for tears, but at last she made a great effort and said, You must look at me and hear what I have to say. For myself I could bear these reproaches, but it is a question of your life; so for your own sake you must listen. I must be able to convince you of my innocence, with so much right on my side.

I would to God you could, he said, but what can you say? Was not M. de Nemours at Coulommiers with his sister? And did he not spend the previous two nights with you in the forest garden?

If this is my crime, she replied, I can easily clear my-self. I don't ask you to believe me, but you must believe the testimony of all your own servants. Find out from them if I went into the forest garden the night before

M. de Nemours came to Coulommiers and whether I did not leave it two hours sooner than I usually do, the night before that.

She went on to tell him how she thought she had seen somebody in the garden, admitting that she had an idea it might be M. de Nemours and speaking with great conviction. Her manner, combined with the fact that truth, even an unlikely truth, is always self-evident, did much to convince M. de Clèves of her innocence.

He said, I don't know whether I ought to believe you . . . I feel so near death that I would almost prefer not to have a reason for wishing to live. This explanation has come too late, though I am glad to depart in the knowledge that you were worthy of my perfect confidence. I should like also to be able to think that you will cherish my memory and that you wanted to feel for me what you felt for that other.

He tried to go on, but he was too weak to say another word. Madame de Clèves sent for the doctors and they found that life was almost extinct; he lingered however a few more days, dying with an admirable firmness of spirit.

MADAME DE CLEVES was almost out of her mind with sorrow. The Queen was very good to her, came to see her and took her to a convent. She went without having any idea where she was; then her sisters-in-law brought her back to Paris before the full force of her grief had broken. But when she was stronger and began to see things more clearly it was borne in upon her what a husband she had lost, and then, realizing that her love for another had killed him, she was seized with an indescribable loathing for herself and for M. de Nemours.

This Prince, in the first stages, did not dare go beyond the usual politenesses, knowing Madame de Clèves quite well enough to know that she would be displeased by any special attentions, but presently he heard something which showed him that he would have to be extremely circumspect for a long time to come. One of his equerries told him that he was great friends with M. de Clèves' gentleman who, distracted with grief, said that his master's death was the direct result of M. de Nemours' visit to Coulommiers. At first this amazed M. de Nemours, but, on thinking it over he guessed more or less what had happened and then he saw exactly what Madame de Clèves' first reactions would be and what a distance there would be between her and him if she really supposed her husband's illness to have been brought on by jealousy. He decided it would be better not even

to bring his name to her attention and followed this course, painful though it was to him.

When he went to Paris, however, he could not resist going to her door and asking for news of her. He was told that she saw nobody and her orders were that she was not to be given the names of her callers—very precise directions which may have been issued with a view to the Prince, so that she should not even hear his name. Now M. de Nemours was far too much in love to be capable of living so absolutely starved of the sight of Madame de Clèves, and he resolved to find a way, however difficult it might be, of putting an end to this unbearable situation.

The Princess's grief went beyond the bounds of reason. Her husband's deathbed preyed on her mind—how he had died because of her and all the time behaving so tenderly to her. She remembered everything she owed him, going over it again and again, and making a crime of not having been passionately in love with him, as though it were a thing she could have helped. Her only consolation was in the thought that she wept him as he deserved, and in resolving to behave, for the rest of her life, as he would have wished had he still been there. She sometimes wondered how it was he knew that M. de Nemours had been to Coulommiers. She did not suspect this Prince of having told it to anybody, but she thought herself so completely cured of her love for him that the whole thing now seemed a matter of supreme indifference. All the same it grieved her that he should have been the cause of her husband's death and she remem-

bered with sorrow how much M. de Clèves, on his deathbed, had worried lest she should marry him. All these things, however, were engulfed in the great sorrow of losing her husband, and she thought that nothing else mattered to her.

Several months went by during which her violent grief gave way to a more passive condition, though she was still very sad. Madame de Martigues, on a visit to Paris, tried to be kind to her, telling all the news from the Court, and though Madame de Clèves seemed quite uninterested she persevered in the hopes of distracting her. She gossiped away about the Vidame, M. de Guise and everybody of interest. And as for M. de Nemours, she said, I can't make out whether it is that politics have taken the place of love affairs, but he certainly is very much less gay than he used to be and seems quite indifferent to women. He comes a great deal to Paris; in fact I believe he is here now.

At the mention of M. de Nemours Madame de Clèves felt a shock; she blushed and changed the subject without Madame de Martigues noticing her agitation.

The next day the Princess, who was always looking out for some suitable occupation, went to see a man in her own neighborhood who did a special kind of work in silk; she thought she could perhaps do something on the same lines herself. After she had been shown everything she noticed a door leading to a room which she had not yet seen, and asked to have it opened. The owner replied that he had not got the key, that the room was occupied by a man who came from time to time, during

daylight, to paint the beautiful houses and gardens which could be seen from the windows.

You never saw such a distinguished man, he went on. Never would one think that he would be obliged to earn a livelihood. He comes here, and I see him gazing at the houses and gardens, but I have never once seen him at work.

Madame de Clèves listened to him with all her ears. The words of Madame de Martigues about M. de Nemours and how he was often in Paris seemed to have a link with this handsome man who came to her own neighborhood. A mental picture of M. de Nemours, determined to see her, rose before her eyes and threw her into an agitation which she could not understand. She went to the windows to see what the view from them might be; it was her own garden and the windows of her own room. Back at home again she easily recognized the window to which, she had been told, the unknown man often came. The thought that this might be M. de Nemours changed her whole outlook upon life; she was shaken from a sort of peaceful melancholy into the throes of restlessness and agitation until, unable to stay quiet any longer, she went out to walk in a garden outside the city where she thought she would be alone. When she got there she saw no sign of life and walked about for quite a long time. Presently she went through a little wood and noticed that there was a kind of summerhouse, open at the sides, at the end of an alley, towards which she directed her steps. When she was quite near it she suddenly saw that there was a man, apparently

deep in reverie, stretched upon one of the benches, and that this man was M. de Nemours. She stopped dead at the sight of him, but the people who were with her made some noise which aroused M. de Nemours from his thoughts. Without looking to see who it was that had made the noise, he got up to avoid the people who were approaching and turned with a low bow which prevented him from seeing whom he thus saluted, up another alley. If only he had known whom it was that he avoided how gladly would he have gone back! But he followed the alley until Madame de Clèves saw him leave by a side entrance where his coach awaited him. The effect which this glimpse of him produced upon Madame de Clèves may well be imagined—her sleeping passion had a violent reawakening. She went to the place where M. de Nemours had been, and sat like one who has been stunned. She suddenly saw the Prince in a new light, as a perfectly adorable being who had loved her long and faithfully, respecting her grief, only wishing to see her without being seen, giving up everything, even a Court of which he was the darling, in order to gaze at the walls of her room and to come and dream in a place where he could hardly hope to meet her—in short, as a man worthy to reign alone in her heart, whom she loved and would have loved even had there been no return; all this, and a person of her own high rank into the bargain. Duty and virtue no longer presented an obstacle to her feelings; nothing that was past could count any more except the love which she and M. de Nemours had for each other.

Such ideas were a novelty to Madame de Clèves, grief over her husband's death having engrossed her whole being until then, but at the sight of M. de Nemours they came over her in force, filling her imagination. After a while, however, she had a powerful reaction. She reminded herself that this man whom she was considering as a possible husband was the cause of her own husband's death, that she had loved him during M. de Clèves' lifetime and that M. de Clèves on his very death-bed had expressed his anxiety lest she should marry him, and all this, so painful to a woman of her character, made her feel that it would be almost as much of a crime to marry M. de Nemours now as it had been to love him during the life of her husband. She fervently embraced these ideas, though they were a death-knell to her happiness, bolstering them up with considerations of her own peace of mind and the various evils which might result from her marriage with this Prince. Two hours later she went home, firmly convinced that it was her duty to shun him for ever.

But this conviction, child of her reason and her virtue, left M. de Nemours in complete possession of her heart —so much so that she was really to be pitied. Sleep was out of the question, and she spent one of the most horrible nights that she had ever known. In the morning her first instinct was to go and see if there was anybody at the window which overlooked her house, and there she saw M. de Nemours. Greatly startled, she withdrew so quickly that the Prince guessed he had been recognized, as indeed he had longed to be ever since his great love

had driven him to find this way of seeing Madame de Clèves. When he gave up hope of seeing her there he used to go and dream in the garden where she had found him.

At last, tired of this sad and unsatisfactory condition, he decided that he must take steps to find out what was to be his fate.

After all, he thought, what am I waiting for? I have known for a long time that she loves me, she is free, it is no longer her duty to keep me at arm's length—why should I be reduced to seeing her like this, without being seen and without speaking with her? Is it possible that I have taken leave of my senses, and lost all initiative? Love has never done that to me before. It was right to respect her grief, but I have respected it for too long altogether, and if I am not careful her feelings for me will begin to fade.

He now began to think how best to approach her, and it occurred to him that as there was no longer any reason for hiding his love from the Vidame de Chartres it would be best to tell him the whole thing, and that he hoped to marry his niece. The Vidame was in Paris, where all the world was preparing carriages and clothes to follow the King, who was to conduct the Queen of Spain to the frontier of her new home. So M. de Nemours went to see the Vidame and confessed everything which he had hitherto kept so secret except that he did not admit his knowledge of Madame de Clèves' feelings for him. The Vidame was overjoyed and said that, though he had no idea M. de Nemours loved her, he had often,

since she had become a widow, thought that she was really the only one good enough to marry him. M. de Nemours asked if he could arrange a meeting, and find out whether she was well disposed towards him. The Vidame then suggested taking him to see her, but M. de Nemours thought she might be shocked by this because she still received nobody. They decided that the Vidame should ask her to go to him, on some pretext or other, and that M. de Nemours should join them secretly, by a special staircase. It all happened as they planned; Madame de Clèves arrived, the Vidame went to receive her and took her to a large room at the end of his apartment. Presently M. de Nemours came in, as though by chance. Madame de Clèves was very much startled to see him; she turned scarlet and tried to conceal the fact. The Vidame chatted away on indifferent subjects and then left them, saying he must give an order about the dinner. He asked Madame de Clèves if she would be good enough to act as hostess for him and added that he would be back very soon.

So, at long last, M. de Nemours and Madame de Clèves found themselves alone and able to speak openly, and their state of mind can be imagined better than it can be described. They said nothing for a while, but at last M. de Nemours broke the silence. You must forgive M. de Chartres, he said, for letting me have an opportunity of seeing you, which you yourself have always so cruelly denied me.

She replied, No, I must not forgive him. He forgets my present situation and that he is endangering my good

name. And she made as if to go away, but M. de Nemours prevented her, saying, You have nothing to fear, Madam, nobody knows that I am here. I implore you to hear what I have to say, if not out of kindness to me then for your own sake, to protect yourself from the follies to which I shall surely be driven by this love I can no longer control.

For the first time Madame de Clèves gave way to her feelings for M. de Nemours and looked at him with a sweet and charming expression.

But what have you to hope for if I consent? she said. You and I will both regret it in the end. You deserve a happier fate than you have had up to now and than you will have in future unless you look elsewhere for it.

Look elsewhere for happiness? he cried. What other happiness can there be except in being loved by you? Although I have never spoken to you, I think you cannot be unaware that my love is true and strong. Heaven knows it has been put to the proof, by you, with your terrible strictness, and by other things you would not understand.

Very well, said Madame de Clèves, sitting down, since you wish me to speak and since I myself have decided to do so I will be perfectly frank with you, more than is usual in a woman. I will not pretend not to have seen that you were in love with me, and perhaps you won't believe me when I say that not only did I see it, but I saw it in the light in which you wanted me to.

He interrupted her to say, And if you really saw it

were you not touched? May I ask whether it did not make some impression on your heart?

That you must judge from my behavior, she replied, and I would be glad to know what you did think of it.

I would not dare speak of that until I am in a happier situation, he said. It has nothing to do with the future. But I am bound to say I could have wished that instead of telling M. de Clèves what you kept from me, you had kept it from him and allowed me to know it.

She blushed and asked him how it was that he knew of her confession to M. de Clèves.

I heard it from your own lips, he replied, but before you condemn my boldness you must consider whether I abused the knowledge in any way, whether it raised my hopes and whether it made me less discreet in my approach. And he began telling her how it was that he had overheard her conversation with M. de Clèves, but she soon interrupted him. Don't go on, she said. I see now why it was that you knew so much—I thought you seemed to be very well informed that day with Madame la Dauphine who had the whole story from the people to whom you had told it.

M. de Nemours told her how this had happened, but she said, You need not make these excuses. I have long ago forgiven you without them. Since you heard from me myself what I meant to keep from you all my life I will now confess that you inspired me with feelings which were not only unknown to me before I saw you but of which I had not even guessed the existence, so that the agitation which they always bring was in my case in-

creased by my great astonishment. I can tell you all this without much shame because it is no longer a crime for me to do so and you know that my behavior has never been influenced by my feelings.

M. de Nemours threw himself at her feet, saying, How can I survive this happiness?

She smiled, and said, I am not telling you anything that you do not already know too well.

Ah! but there is a difference between finding out by an accident and being told by you yourself, of your own free will, glad that I should know.

Quite true, she said. I am glad that you should know and there is a certain sweetness in telling you—so much so that perhaps I do it more for my own sake than for yours. When all's said and done this confession will be without consequences, and I shall follow the lines, austere though they be, laid down by my duty.

But you are free now, cried M. de Nemours. Duty no longer enters into the question—indeed if I might make so bold I would ask you to put yourself in a position in which your first duty would be to cherish these feelings for me.

My duty, she replied, forbids me ever to think of any man, and of you less than anybody in the world, for reasons which are unknown to you.

Perhaps not entirely unknown, but your reasons are not valid. It would seem that M. de Clèves supposed me luckier than in fact I was and imagined that you had approved of certain extravagances which I committed,

driven to them by my great love and without knowing whether or not it was requited.

Don't, please, remind me of that episode, she said. I only want to forget it—I can't think of it without shame and deepest grief for the consequences. The plain truth is that the suspicions you aroused by your utterly thoughtless behavior are as much responsible for my husband's death as if you had killed him with your own hands. Supposing you had done so, you know what my duty would be—oh, in the eyes of the world it is not the same, I am quite well aware of that, but to me there is no difference at all; I know that you were the cause of his death, and on my account.

Alas, said M. de Nemours, what is this phantom of duty which you are placing between me and my happiness? A vain thought, based on air, is to keep you from making the joy of a man whom you do not hate. My lucky star leads me to fall in love with the most estimable lady in the world, I see hopes of spending my life with her, she does not hate me, and in her I see the combination of all that can make a perfect mistress and a perfect wife. Indeed, I suppose that you must be the only person who has ever so completely combined the qualities necessary to both. Those who marry the mistresses by whom they are loved do so in fear and trembling, measuring their future behavior in terms of the past, but in your case there is nothing to fear since whichever way one looks at your behavior the causes for admiration can only be multiplied. Must such great felicity lie within my grasp and must I then see you yourself raising these obstacles? Was

it not you who distinguished me above all men? Were you mistaken? Or did I merely flatter myself that it was so?

You did not flatter yourself at all, she replied, and it is quite possible that the reasons for what seems to be my duty would not be insuperable were it not that I do so distinguish you. That is what makes me feel that loving you can only end in unhappiness for me.

Now what can I say? So unhappiness is all you anticipate? I had hardly expected to have such a cruel reason put forward after all you have been good enough to tell me.

And yet there is nothing offensive to you in it, replied Madame de Clèves, so much the contrary that I find it quite difficult to explain what I mean.

Indeed! And what is this flattering thing that you are so frightened of?

I shall go on speaking quite openly, she said, and without the shades of reserve that I ought perhaps to maintain during our very first conversation. So please to listen without interrupting me. Your love for me seems to deserve that I should let you see my own feelings exactly as they are; it is the least that I can do. I suppose that this is the only time in my life when I shall allow myself to show you just what I do feel; nevertheless it is not without shame that I make this confession. The fact is that I dare not expose myself to the misery of seeing your love grow cold. It is sure to happen; it seems to me the most terrible of fates, and, since it is not my duty to risk it I feel that I cannot do so. You are free. I am free. People may not have

any reasons for censuring either of us if we decide to spend the rest of our days together, but in these eternal relationships does any man preserve his original passion? Can I expect a miracle in my case? And dare I put myself in a position whence I shall be obliged to witness the death of a love in which lies all my joy? There was perhaps one man and one man only capable of being in love with his wife, and that was M. de Clèves. It was my bad luck that this brought me no happiness—possibly this passion of his would not have continued so strong if I had requited it, but I cannot use that means for keeping yours. Then I have an idea that it was the obstacles which kept you so true to me; there were enough of them to rouse your mettle, while my involuntary actions and the various things you found out by chance gave you the necessary amount of hope to sustain you.

Really I cannot keep silent any longer, said M. de Nemours. You are being too unfair to me and showing only too plainly that you are very far from being predisposed in my favor.

I confess, she said, that I can be led by my passions, but they have never blinded me and I cannot help knowing that you are a born lover, with every attribute that makes for success; you have already been in love several times and will be again. I should not make you happy; I should see you with somebody else as you had been with me, and it would strike me to the heart, defenseless as I am against jealousy. I have said too much to conceal from you that I have felt this jealousy already; indeed, I suffered so terribly the evening when the Queen gave me Mad-

ame de Thémine's letter, which was supposed to be yours, that I know it for the worst of all evils.

Every woman alive, whether from love or vanity, longs to make a conquest of you; there are very few who do not feel your charm. Indeed it seems to me, from my own experience, that you can attract whom you please. I should always imagine you as loved and loving, and should seldom be mistaken, and then there would be nothing for me to do but suffer; I should not even dare to complain. A lover can be reproached but what can be said to a husband whose only fault is having ceased to love? I might get used to it I suppose, but could I ever get used to thinking I see M. de Clèves accusing you of having killed him, reproaching me for loving and having married you and making me feel the difference between his love and yours? Here are reasons which admit of no argument and I am resolved to go on as I am now for ever and ever.

Yes, but will you be able to? cried M. de Nemours. Do you really think such resolutions are much good against a man who worships you and who is fortunate enough to attract you? It is perhaps more difficult than you know to put up a resistance to love. So far you have succeeded by means of an unexampled virtue, but your present feelings have nothing to do with virtue and I am hoping that, in spite of yourself, they will win the day.

I realize that nothing could be more difficult than to carry out my decision, said Madame de Clèves, and I might be doubtful of my power to do so, were it not for my reasons. The duty I owe to M. de Clèves' memory

would, in itself, be too weak, were it not reinforced by considerations of my own peace of mind. My peace of mind in its turn is reinforced by duty. I may be unsure of myself but I think my scruples are invincible for, though never shall I be able to overcome my inclination for you, I know that to indulge it would end in too much unhappiness. So I am not going to see you again, whatever it costs me, and I conjure you by all the power I have over you not to try to see me. In my present state of mind things which would ordinarily seem permissible become magnified into crimes; decency forbids that we should see each other.

Now M. de Nemours lost all his self-control. He threw himself at her feet and bore witness by his words and his tears to as lively and tender a passion as has ever been felt by human heart. That of Madame de Clèves being not quite insensitive she said, as she looked at the Prince, his eyes all swollen with tears, Oh why am I obliged to lay my husband's death at your door? Why could I not have met you since I have been free or before I became engaged? Why must there be so insurmountable a barrier between us?

There is no such barrier, replied M. de Nemours, except in your own imagination. You have put yourself between me and my happiness, inventing a law which neither virtue nor sense would have imposed upon you.

Yes, I am indeed sacrificing much to a duty which only exists in my own imagination, she said. Wait a little; see what time may do. M. de Clèves has only just died; all this is too near for me to see it in a proper perspective.

Take what pleasure you can in the thought that you have awakened love in one who would never have known what it meant had she never seen you. You must believe that the feelings I have for you will never change whatever my actions may be. Adieu. I am ashamed of this conversation but please give an account of it to M. le Vidame. I allow you to; I even ask you to do so.

ON these words she left M. de Nemours; he could not stop her. She found M. le Vidame in the next room; he saw that she was deeply upset, and did not dare speak, but accompanied her to her carriage in silence. He went back to M. de Nemours whom he found out of his mind with joy, misery, and an amazed admiration—in short, all the feelings that there are in a passion which knows not whether to hope or to despair. It was a long time before the Vidame could make head or tail of the conversation they had had; but when finally he understood everything he felt, though not in love with her, as much admiration for Madame de Clèves, for her virtue, her spirit and her general worth, as M. de Nemours did himself. They talked the matter over, weighing M. de Nemours' chances of success and he, in spite of an anxiety which really came from being so much in love, agreed with M. le Vidame that Madame de Clèves would never be able to keep to her resolution. They decided however that he had better do as she wished lest people should notice his feelings for her and that she, fearing that it would be said she had loved him during her husband's life, should take a certain line of action which later on she might feel obliged to maintain.

M. de Nemours now decided to travel with the King, since in any case it would have been difficult for him to get out of that journey, and to go without attempting to

see Madame de Clèves again, even from the place where he had sometimes watched her. He asked the Vidame to speak to her for him, pouring out a hundred things which he was to say—a hundred reasons why she must overcome her scruples; indeed, the night was well advanced before it occurred to him that his friend might want to go to bed.

There was no peace for Madame de Clèves that night. After all, this had been the first time she had left her self-imposed retreat as well as the first time she had ever allowed anybody to make a declaration of love to her; added to which, she herself had now admitted to being in love. She did not recognize herself anymore. She was amazed to think what she had done, and, not knowing whether to be glad or sorry, her mind was filled with a passionate restlessness. She went over the reasons which duty seemed to put between her and her happiness, and found, to her sorrow, that they were very powerful; she wished now that she had not described them so lucidly to M. de Nemours. Although she had conceived the idea of marrying him as soon as she saw him in the garden it was only brought home to her by their conversation. Now she had moments when she found it hard to believe that such a marriage would make her unhappy, so much did she long to be able to think that this idea was founded on a misapprehension of past scruples and fears for the future. Duty and good sense seemed to point first one way and then another, but all paths led to a final resolution—not to remarry and never to see M. de Nemours again. It was not easy to reconcile her heart to this, deeply affected

as it was and given over for the first time to the delights of love; so, seeking a little respite, she told herself that she need not force herself just yet to a final decision, since the very proprieties demanded that she should take her time. But she was perfectly decided to be firm about not seeing M. de Nemours.

The Vidame came to see her and did what he could for M. de Nemours, putting his heart and soul into the matter, but without success. She would not relax either her own behavior or that which she had imposed upon M. de Nemours. She told the Vidame that she intended to remain as she was, that she knew this would be far from easy but that she hoped to find the strength for it. He realized now her certitude both of M. de Nemours' responsibility for her husband's death and that it was her absolute duty not to marry him, so much so that he saw it would be very difficult to remove this conviction.

However, when repeating the talk he had had with her to the Duke he did not add his own reflections but left him in the not unreasonable optimism of a man who knows himself beloved.

Next day they went off to join the King. M. le Vidame wrote to Madame de Clèves, at the request of M. de Nemours, speaking of this Prince, and to a second letter, which quickly followed the first, M. de Nemours added a few lines in his own hand. But Madame de Clèves, who was determined to keep to the rules she herself had laid down and who dreaded the various mishaps which letters can bring in their train, sent word to the Vidame that she could not receive any more from him if

he continued to speak of M. de Nemours. She made such a point of this that M. de Nemours himself asked the Vidame not to mention him again.

The Court was to accompany the Queen of Spain as far as Poitou. During this absence Madame de Clèves was quite alone and the further removed she felt from M. de Nemours and all the things which could remind her of him the more she cherished the memory of M. de Clèves. Her reasons against marrying M. de Nemours now seemed insurmountable both with regard to her duty and her peace of mind. She thought it quite sure that marriage would put an end to his love and expose her to all the horrors of jealousy and that she would therefore be delivering herself up to certain unhappiness if she married him, but she also realized that it would be impossible to resist this charming man she loved so much if she went on seeing him, especially as neither virtue nor decency demanded that she should do so. She saw that absence alone could fortify her; she needed it, not only if she were to keep her resolution to enter into no engagement, but also to prevent her from meeting M. de Nemours. She therefore decided upon a fairly long journey so that she could be quite alone for the rest of the time she was in mourning. A large estate she owned near the Pyrenees seemed the best place, and a few days before the Court was to return to Paris she started off. Before leaving she wrote and begged M. le Vidame that nobody should write to her or try to have news of her.

M. de Nemours felt this journey as another might feel the death of his mistress. Having had the happiness of

seeing Madame de Clèves and of knowing that his love had affected her it was a great blow to be deprived of her presence for so long. There was nothing to be done, but he was sadder than ever. As for Madame de Clèves, the stresses and strains were too much for her and as soon as she arrived at her house she became very ill. This news duly reached the Court; M. de Nemours could not be consoled. His grief became quite exaggerated and the Vidame had all the trouble in the world to prevent him from parading it in front of everybody and from going himself to find out how she was. As M. le Vidame was a relation and close friend it was natural for him to send messengers; at last they heard that the immediate danger was over but that she had gone into a decline and there was not much hope that she would live.

With death so near her for so long Madame de Clèves' ideas had changed very much and she saw the world and all that pertains to it with an eye which can never be the same as that of good health. Feeling sure that she would die she became perfectly detached, a state of mind which the length of her illness turned into a habit. Later on, when she was more herself again, she found that though the image of M. de Nemours had by no means faded in her heart, the arguments against the marriage now seemed conclusive, and after an inner struggle of some violence she succeeded in smothering the remains of her passion. The nearness of death had given her a new perspective of this earthly life, its appetites and entanglements assuming but meager proportions, while the memory of M. de Clèves, with its implied reproaches, now

loomed very large. She remained delicate in health, and this made it easier to keep to her resolve, but knowing too well how quickly the sincerest intentions can be overthrown by circumstances she was determined not to make things more difficult by going back to places connected with her love. She went into a nunnery, giving out that she needed a change of air, but not making any announcement about retiring from the Court.

As soon as M. de Nemours heard of this he saw that it was a significant move, and he felt it terribly. In fact it now seemed to him that he had no more to hope for, though this presentiment did not stop him from doing his utmost to bring back Madame de Clèves. He made the Queen write to her; he made the Vidame write, and go to see her—in vain. When the Vidame saw her she did not mention that she had quite made up her mind, but all the same he felt sure that she would never come back. Finally M. de Nemours went himself under pretext of taking some waters. She was deeply troubled and surprised to hear that he had arrived. She had with her a trustworthy person whom she loved, and sent word by her that she begged him not to think it strange of her if she did not expose herself to the danger of seeing him and of having her present state of mind, which seemed right to her, destroyed by his presence. She wanted him to know that, since to give way to her feeling for him would be fatal to her inward peace, as well as contrary to her duty, she had renounced the world, which no longer held anything for her, and had fixed her thoughts upon the

world to come. Her only wish now was to see him in the same state.

M. de Nemours thought he would die of grief in the presence of the woman who told him all this. Twenty times he besought her to go back to Madame de Clèves and arrange somehow for him to see her, but she told him that Madame de Clèves had not only forbidden her to bring any message from him but even to give her any account of their conversation. So at last this Prince was obliged to go away, overcome with sorrow, as indeed well he might be—he who could never again hope to see the lady he loved so violently, and with such good cause. Even now he would not give up, and did everything imaginable to make her change her mind. At last, after the passage of whole years, his love and his grief became less acute. Madame de Clèves gave no sign of ever returning to the world. She spent a part of each year in the convent and the rest of it at home, but living in an even greater austerity, with even holier occupations than in the strictest of orders. Indeed her life, which was not a long one, provided an example of inimitable goodness.

NOTES TO THE PRINCESS OF CLEVES

BRISSAC, Marechal de, 1505–1563. Created Marshal of France in 1550.

BUSSY-RABUTIN, Roger de, 1618–1693. Wit and writer, cousin of Madame de Sévigné. Exiled by Louis XIV to his castle of Bussy le Grand.

CARLOS, Don, 1545–1568. Son of Philip II of Spain. He was very unbalanced and died mysteriously in prison.

CATHERINE DE MEDICIS, 1529–1589. Wife of Henri II, mother of François II, Charles IX and Henri III. Her daughter, Margot, was the first wife of Henri IV.

CHARTRES, Francois de Vendome, Vidame de, 1522–1560. He is thought to have been poisoned by order of Catherine de Medicis whose love he had rejected.

CHATELART. According to Brantôme he was madly in love with Mary Stuart, and was executed after being found hiding in her bedroom. Swinburne wrote a poem about this.

CLEVES, Jacques, Prince de, died in 1564. Second son of the first Duc de Nevers. He never married.

CONDE, Louis de Bourbon, Prince de, 1530–1569. Uncle of Henri IV and founder of the Condé

branch of the Bourbon family. He was assassinated by an agent of the Duc d'Anjou.

COULANGES, MARQUIS DE, 1613–1671. Cousin of Madame de Sévigné. He composed charming songs. His wife wrote letters (see bibliography of Mme. de Lafayette) and was a beauty.

ELIZABETH OF FRANCE, 1545–1568. Daughter of Henri II. She seems to have been very happy with Philip of Spain. Madame de Lafayette, when speaking of her fatal beauty, refers to a legend that she had a love affair with her step-son Don Carlos, but there is absolutely no foundation for this story.

FERRARA, ALPHONSO D'ESTE, DUKE OF. Cousin of Henri II. Brother of the Duchesse de Guise who married (her second marriage), the Duc de Nemours and may have been the original for the Princesse de Clèves.

FRANCOIS II OF FRANCE, 1543–1560. Married Mary Stuart Queen of Scots in 1558, came to the throne at the death of his father Henri II in 1559 but was too ill to reign.

GUISE, CARDINAL CHARLES DE LORRAINE, 1524–1574. Brother of the Duc de Guise and uncle of Mary Stuart.

GUISE, FRANCOIS DE LORRAINE, CHEVALIER DE, died in 1562. He accompanied Mary Stuart to Scotland in 1561. He also led an expedition to Rhodes, and was killed at the battle of Dreux.

GUISE, FRANCOIS DE LORRAINE, DUC DE, 1519–1563. Governed on behalf of François II during his short

reign. Assassinated by a Huguenot. His widow married the Duc de Nemours.

HENRI II OF FRANCE, 1519–1559. Son of François I and Queen Claude. A patron of the arts and a brave soldier, but a poor administrator. He was accidentally killed by the Comte de Montgoméry in a tournament. The monument to him and Catherine de Medicis at Saint-Denis survived the French revolution and is one of the glories of the French Renaissance.

HENRIETTA, PRINCESS OF ENGLAND, Duchesse d'Orléans, 1644–1670.

HUET, Pierre Daniel, Bishop of Avranches, 1630–1721.

LAFAYETTE, Francois Comte de, 1616–1682. He owned properties at La Fayette, Médat, Gontevanteouze, Chouvigny, Espinasse, Nades, Hauteserre and Hautefeuille.

LAFAYETTE, Louise de, 1615–1665. Abbesse of the Convent of Chaillot, formerly lady in waiting to Anne of Austria, wife of Louis XIII.

LOUVOIS, Michel le Tellier, Marquis de, 1641–1691. Founder of the modern French army. It was at his suggestion that Louis XIV built the Invalides. Died of overwork.

LORRAINE, Charles, Duc de, 1543–1608. Married Claude, daughter of Henri II.

MARGUERITE DE FRANCE, "Madame, the King's Sister," 1525–1574. Daughter of François I.

MARY STUART, 1542–1587. Queen of Scots in her own right, married in 1558 the Dauphin of France. She returned to Scotland, a widow, in 1561.

MAZARIN, Cardinal, 1602–1661. Born in Italy, naturalized French in 1639. Ruled France from the death of Richelieu during the minority of Louis XIV over whom he always had great influence. Louis XIV wanted to marry Marie Mancini, Mazarin's niece, but Mazarin would not hear of it and arranged the Spanish alliance. Not until his death did Louis XIV take over absolute power.

MENAGE, the Abbe Gilles, 1613–1692.

MERCŒUR, Jeanne de Savoie, Duchesse de. Sister of the Duc de Nemours.

MIGNARD, Nicholas, 1606–1668. Court painter of Louis XIV. He did much decorative work at the Tuilleries.

MONTGOMERY, Gabriel, Comte de, 1530–1574. Captain of Henri II's Scottish Regiment.

MONTMORENCY, Anne, Duc de, 1492–1567. Connétable de France, a title which was more or less hereditary in his enormously powerful family, the owners of Chantilly. He was killed at Saint Denis fighting against Calvinists.

NAVARRE, Antoine de Bourbon, King of, 1518–1562. Father of Henri IV of France.

NAVARRE, Marguerite, Queen of, 1492–1549. Sister of François I.

NEMOURS, Jacques de Savoie, Duc de, 1531–1585. Married Anne d'Este, widow of the Duc de Guise. See Introduction.

NEVERS, Francois de Cleves, Duc de, 1516–1562. Father of the Prince de Clèves.

ORLEANS, Philippe, Duc de, 1640–1701. Founder of the existing Orléans family. Married first Princess Henrietta of England, second Charlotte Elizabeth, 1652–1722, daughter of the Elector of Palatine, by whom he had one son, Philippe, Regent of France.

RETZ, Jean Francois Paul de Gondi, Cardinal de, 1613–1679. He wrote an account of the Fronde which is invaluable to historians.

ROCHEFOUCAULD, Francois, Duc de la, 1613–1680.

SAINT ANDRE, Jacques d'Albon, Marechal de. Killed at the battle of Dreux.

SEGRAIS, Jean de, 1624–1701.

SEVIGNE, Marquise de, 1626–1696.

THIANGES, Marquise de, died in 1693. Daughter of the Duc de Mortemart.

VALENTINOIS, Diane de Poitiers, Duchesse de, 1499–1566. Everything that Madame de Lafayette says about her extraordinary career is perfectly true.

THE REVIVED MODERN CLASSICS

H.E. Bates
A Month by the Lake & Other Stories. Introduction by Anthony Burgess. Seventeen stories by the English master (1905–1974): "without an equal in England in the kind of story he made his own." — *London Times.* Cloth & NDPaperbook 645. *A Party for the Girls.* Six long stories by "the Renoir of the typewriter." — *Punch.* Cloth & NDP653. *Elephant's Nest in a Rhubarb Tree.* More stories by the "so gifted...contemporary and worthy colleague of Evelyn Waugh and Graham Greene." — *N.Y. Times Book Review.* Cloth & NDP669.

Kay Boyle
Death of a Man. Novel set in fascist Austria: "all the elegance...No sentimentality—a painful dose of the early poisons that tasted so sweet." — Grace Paley. NDP670. *Life Being the Best and Other Stories.* Edited by S. W. Spanier. Thirteen early stories. "Boyle's writing captures the moment of visionary realism when sensation heightens and time for an instant fixes and stops." — Margaret Atwood. Cloth & NDP654.

Mikhail Bulgakov
The Life of Monsieur de Molière. Trans. by Mirra Ginsburg. A vivid portrait of the great French 17th-century satirist by one of the great Russian satirists of our own century. Cloth & NDP601.

Joyce Cary
"Second Trilogy": *Prisoner of Grace. Except the Lord. Not Honour More.* "Even better than Cary's 'First Trilogy,' this is one of the great political novels of this century." — *San Francisco Examiner.* NDP606, 607, & 608. *A House of Children.* Reprint of the delightful autobiographical novel. NDP631. *Mister Johnson.* Novel: "[It] illustrates one of the rarest miracles that literature is capable of: that inexplicable process by which the intellectually simple becomes the emotionally dense, by which stereotype becomes archetype." — *N.Y. Review of Books.* NDP657.

Maurice Collis
The Land of the Great Image. "A vivid and illuminating study written with the care and penetration that an artist as well as a historian must exercise to make the exotic past live and breathe for us." — Eudora Welty. NDP612.

Ronald Firbank
Three More Novels. "An inexhaustible source of pleasure."—*The Village Voice Literary Supplement*. NDP614.

Romain Gary
The Life Before Us (Madame Rosa). Trans. by Ralph Manheim. "You won't forget Momo and Madame Rosa when you close the book. *The Life Before Us* is a moving reading experience, if you don't mind a good cry."—*St. Louis Post-Dispatch*. NDP604. *Promise at Dawn*. A memoir "bursting with life…Gary's art has been to combine the comic and the tragic."—*The New Yorker*. NDP635.

Henry Green
Back. "A rich, touching story, flecked all over by Mr. Green's intuition of the concealed orginality of ordinary human beings."—V. S. Pritchett. NDP517.

Madame de Lafayette
The Princess of Cleves. A great work of French literature and perhaps the first of all "modern" novels. "Nancy Mitford, a delicately devastating observer of the aristocracy herself, is an ideal selection as the translator."—Virginia Kirkus. "One of the most charming things."—Mme. de Sévignè. NDP660.

Siegfried Lenz
The German Lesson. Trans. by Ernst Kaiser and Eithne Wilkins. "A book of rare depth and brilliance…"—*The New York Times*. NDP618.

Henri Michaux
A Barbarian in Asia. Trans. by Sylvia Beach. "It is superb in its swift illuminations and its wit…"—Alfred Kazin, *The New Yorker*. NDP622.

Raymond Queneau
The Blue Flowers. Trans. by Barbara Wright. Novel. A medieval duke and a 1960s Parisian barge dweller romp through history: "inventive, word-mad, and funny…"—*The Washington Post*. "Queneau is one of those cerebral magicians who sparkles like a black pearl."—*Booklist*. NDP595.

Kenneth Rexroth
Classics Revisited. Sixty brief, radiant essays on the books Rexroth called the "basic documents in the history of the imagination." NDP621. *More*

Classics Revisited. Ed. by Bradford Morrow. More succinct essays by "one of a vanishing race of giants, a literary lion."—Andrei Codrescu. "Anyone who wants to be globally literate...could ask for no better guide than this."—*Booklist*. Cloth & NDP668.

William Saroyan
The Man with the Heart in the Highlands & Other Early Stories. "Probably since O. Henry nobody has done more to endear and stabilize the short story."—Elizabeth Bowen. Cloth.

Robert Penn Warren
At Heaven's Gate. A novel of power and corruption in the deep South of the 1920s. "Great poetic intensity."—*The Sewanee Review*. NDP588.